AF207164

REXTOOTH STUDIOS

50 MILLION YEARS OF
WHALES

WRITTEN & ILLUSTRATED BY **TED RECHLIN**

EDITED BY **ANNE RECHLIN**

PUBLISHED BY REXTOOTH STUDIOS, BOZEMAN, MONTANA

PRODUCED BY SWEETGRASS BOOKS, HELENA, MONTANA

ISBN: 978-1-59152-273-7

COVER DESIGN BY TED RECHLIN

PRINTED IN CHINA

THE BLUE WHALE IS THE LARGEST ANIMAL EVER TO LIVE ON PLANET EARTH.

100 FEET LONG AND WEIGHING UP TO 190 TONS –

ITS HEART ALONE WEIGHS AS MUCH AS AN AFRICAN LION.

THIS IS A CREATURE OF *SUPER* PROPORTIONS.
AND, LIKE ALL THINGS SUPER –
THERE IS A SPECTACULAR *ORIGIN STORY* TO BE TOLD.

375 MILLION YEARS AGO
EONS AGO, SOME FISH TURNED THEIR FINS INTO LEGS AND COLONIZED THE LAND.
EVOLUTION TURNED THEM INTO THE FOUR-LIMBED TETRAPODS.
REPTILES.
THROUGHOUT THE MESOZOIC - MORE THAN 180 MILLION YEARS - REPTILES REIGNED.
FLYING REPTILES SOARED THE SKIES.
OTHERS RETURNED TO DOMINATE THE SEA.

THEY BECAME AMPHIBIANS, SYNAPSIDS, MAMMALS –
AND *DINOSAURS* RULED THE EARTH.
UNTIL THE *COSMOS* PUT AN END TO THE *AGE OF REPTILES*.
66 MILLION YEARS AGO

TO SET THE STAGE FOR A NEW ACT, A CURTAIN MUST FALL ON THE ONE BEFORE.

FROM THE ASHES OF THE MESOZOIC, MAMMALS WOULD RISE TO CLAIM THE SPOTLIGHT.

50 MILLION YEARS AGO
PAKISTAN
15 MILLION YEARS AFTER THE END OF THE AGE OF REPTILES, THE EARTH IS RENEWED.
HERE, A SMALL ANIMAL - A MAMMAL - FORAGES FOR FOOD.
SNIFF
SHE'S CALLED INDOHYUS.
WOOOOO

SHE'S ABOUT THE SIZE OF A HOUSE CAT, AND LOOKS KIND OF LIKE A *COMPRESSED* DEER.

AND SHE'S IN *DANGER.*

HER PURSUER IS A DOG-SIZED CARNIVORE CALLED A MESONYCHID.

INDOHYUS IS QUICK.
DEAD END.
SPLASH
HRMPH

BUT SO IS HER PURSUER.
THERE IS NO ESCAPE.
UNLESS...
?

BOTH INDOHYUS AND THE MESONYCHID ARE EARLY ANCESTORS OF A GROUP OF ANIMALS CALLED ARTIODACTYLS.

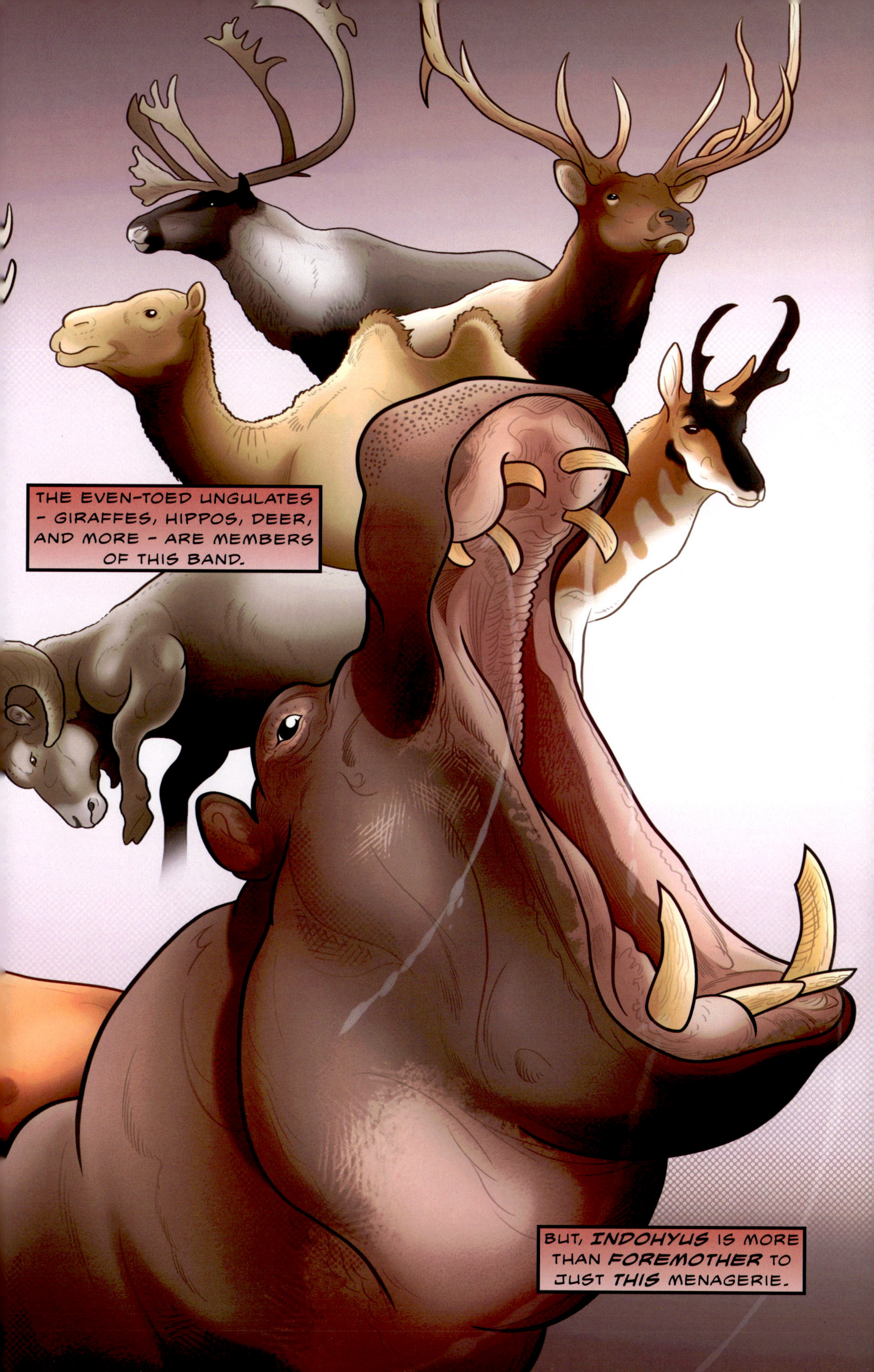

THE EVEN-TOED UNGULATES - GIRAFFES, HIPPOS, DEER, AND MORE - ARE MEMBERS OF THIS BAND.
BUT, INDOHYUS IS MORE THAN FOREMOTHER TO JUST THIS MENAGERIE.

INDOHYUS HAS HEAVY BONES THAT ALLOW HER TO SINK —
AND SHE'S GREAT AT HOLDING HER BREATH.
SHE'S ALSO GOT SPECIALIZED EAR BONES THAT HELP HER HEAR BETTER UNDERWATER.
IT'S A SET OF *SUPER POWERS* THAT SHE USES TO ESCAPE FROM PREDATORS.
THESE MAKE HER A *KEY* LINK IN AN EVOLUTIONARY *CHAIN*.

BELIEVE IT OR NOT, OUR MODERN WHALES' CLOSEST RELATIVES ARE THE ARTIODACTYLS.
AND INDOHYUS, AN UNGULATE WITH SPECIAL ADAPTATIONS FOR LIFE UNDERWATER, IS A BRIDGE BETWEEN THE TWO GROUPS.

2 MILLION YEARS LATER

INDOHYUS DEBUTED NEW FEATURES - HEAVY BONES AND SPECIAL *HEAR-UNDERWATER-EARS* - THIS WOLF-SIZED ANIMAL CAPITALIZES ON THEM.

THIS IS PAKICETUS.

327 MILLION YEARS EARLIER,
SEA CREATURES BECAME
LAND-DWELLERS.

NOW, PAKICETUS RETURNS TO THE WATER.
HE SPENDS MOST OF HIS TIME ON LAND, BUT THERE'S *LOTS* TO EAT BENEATH THE RIPPLES.
HE'S NOT THE MOST *GRACEFUL* SWIMMER –
NONETHELESS, HE IS THE FIRST OF A GROUP CALLED THE *CETACEANS.*
HE IS THE VERY FIRST *WHALE.*

WHEN WE THINK OF ANIMALS THAT SPLIT THEIR LIVES BETWEEN LAND AND WATER, CROCODILIANS COME TO MIND.
THEY ARE SLEEK-BODIED, STEALTHY PREDATORS.
BUT, THROUGHOUT LIFE ON EARTH, OTHER ANIMALS HAVE ADOPTED THIS BODY-STYLE, AND PUT IT TO SIMILAR USE.

IT'S A PHENOMENON CALLED CONVERGENT EVOLUTION.

47 MILLION YEARS AGO

THESE SMALL HORSES ARE EAGER TO QUENCH THEIR THIRST ON A HOT DAY.

BUT THE WATER'S CALM SURFACE IS A LIE.

JUST LIKE A CROCODILE LUNGING FOR A WILDEBEEST, AMBULOCETUS SURGES TOWARD ITS PREY.
THIS EQUINE'S REFLEXES ARE NOT FAST ENOUGH.

AMBULOCETUS IS A *500-POUND* MAMMAL THAT HUNTS LIKE A CROCODILE.

AND, LIKE A CROCODILE, IT DOESN'T LIVE ITS WHOLE LIFE IN THE WATER.

"AMBULOCETUS," AFTER ALL, TRANSLATES TO "WALKING WHALE."

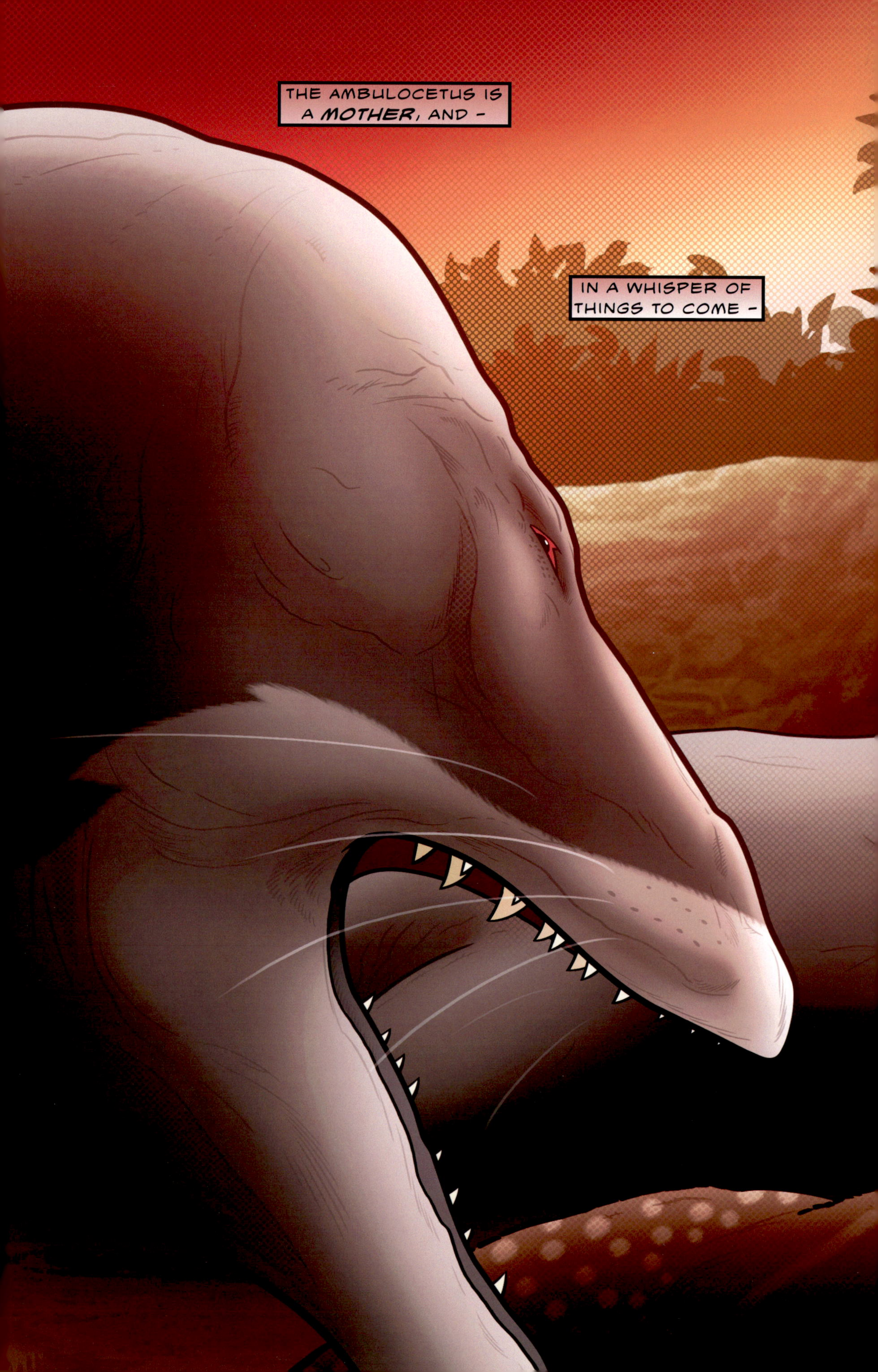

THE AMBULOCETUS IS A MOTHER, AND –
IN A WHISPER OF THINGS TO COME –

THIS EARLY WHALE HAS A FAMILY.

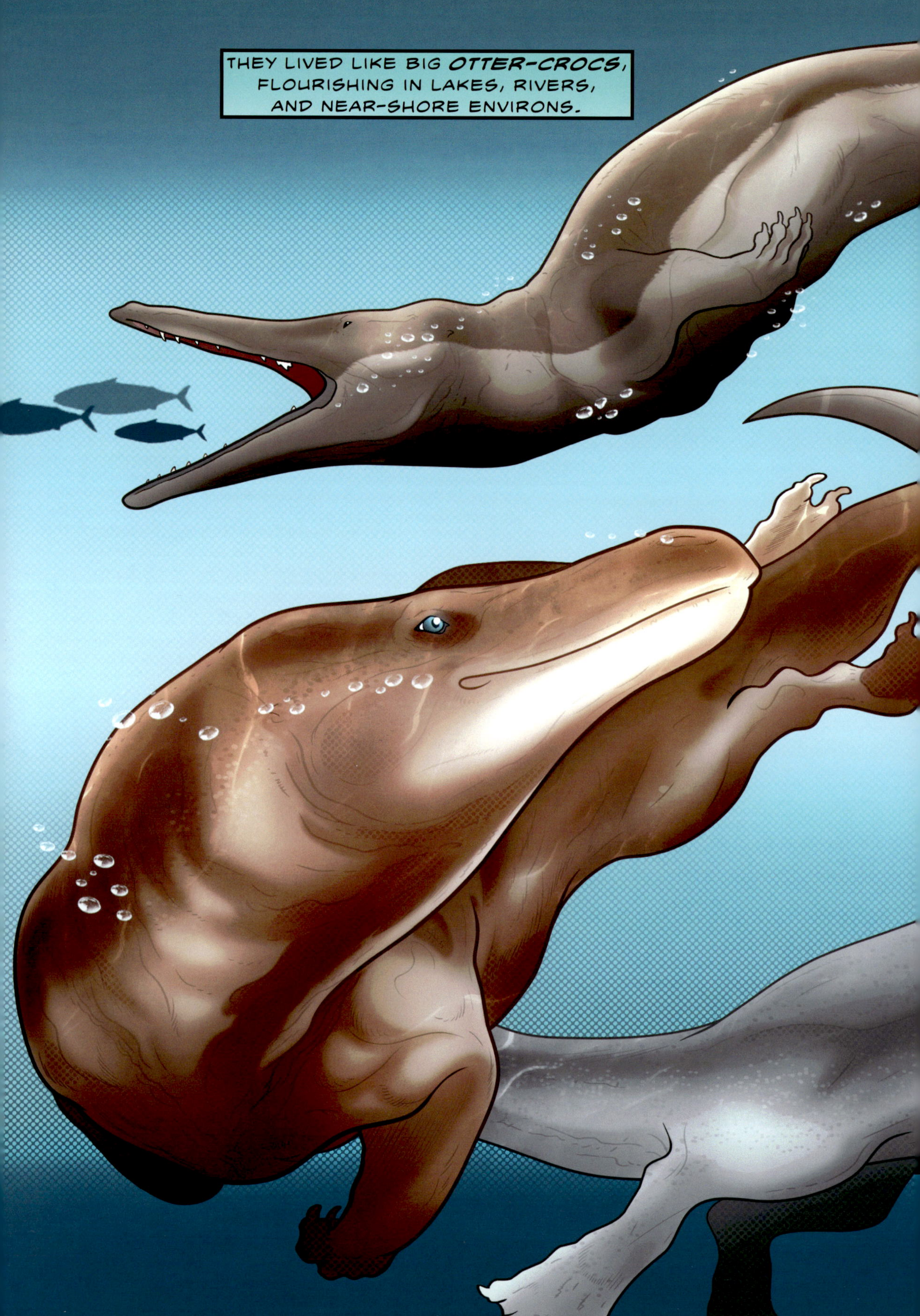
FOR A FEW MILLION YEARS, AMBULOCETUS AND ITS EARLY-CETACEAN RELATIVES DID WELL FOR THEMSELVES.
THEY LIVED LIKE BIG OTTER-CROCS, FLOURISHING IN LAKES, RIVERS, AND NEAR-SHORE ENVIRONS.

BUT THEY COULDN'T CONQUER THE *OPEN OCEANS* LIKE THIS.

THE OCEANS WERE A DANGEROUS PLACE FOR THE SEAL-SIZED WHALES.

TO SURVIVE THE BIG MOVE, THE CETACEANS WOULD HAVE TO MAKE SOME BIG CHANGES.

THE SEAS, AFTER ALL,
WERE HOME TO
MONSTERS...

IN THE 1800'S, THE BONES OF A MASSIVE SEA CREATURE WERE DISCOVERED.
SCIENTISTS THOUGHT THE BONES BELONGED TO A REPTILE, A RELATIVE OF THE MOSASAURS AND PLESIOSAURS OF THE MESOZOIC.
THEY NAMED THIS SEA SERPENT, BASILOSAURUS.

AS IT TURNS OUT, THEY WERE...
NOT QUITE RIGHT.

37 MILLION YEARS AGO
THIS IS BASILOSAURUS.
WITH A MOUTH FULL OF TEETH MADE FOR STABBING AND CRUSHING, IT'S NOT A SEA SERPENT –
THOUGH IT'S NO LESS FEARSOME.
THOUGH ORIGINALLY MISIDENTIFIED, BASILOSAURUS WAS ACTUALLY THE FIRST FOSSIL WHALE KNOWN TO SCIENCE.
THIS CETACEAN HAS FLIPPERS INSTEAD OF FEET.

AND IT IS THE *TOP* OF THE OCEANIC FOOD CHAIN.

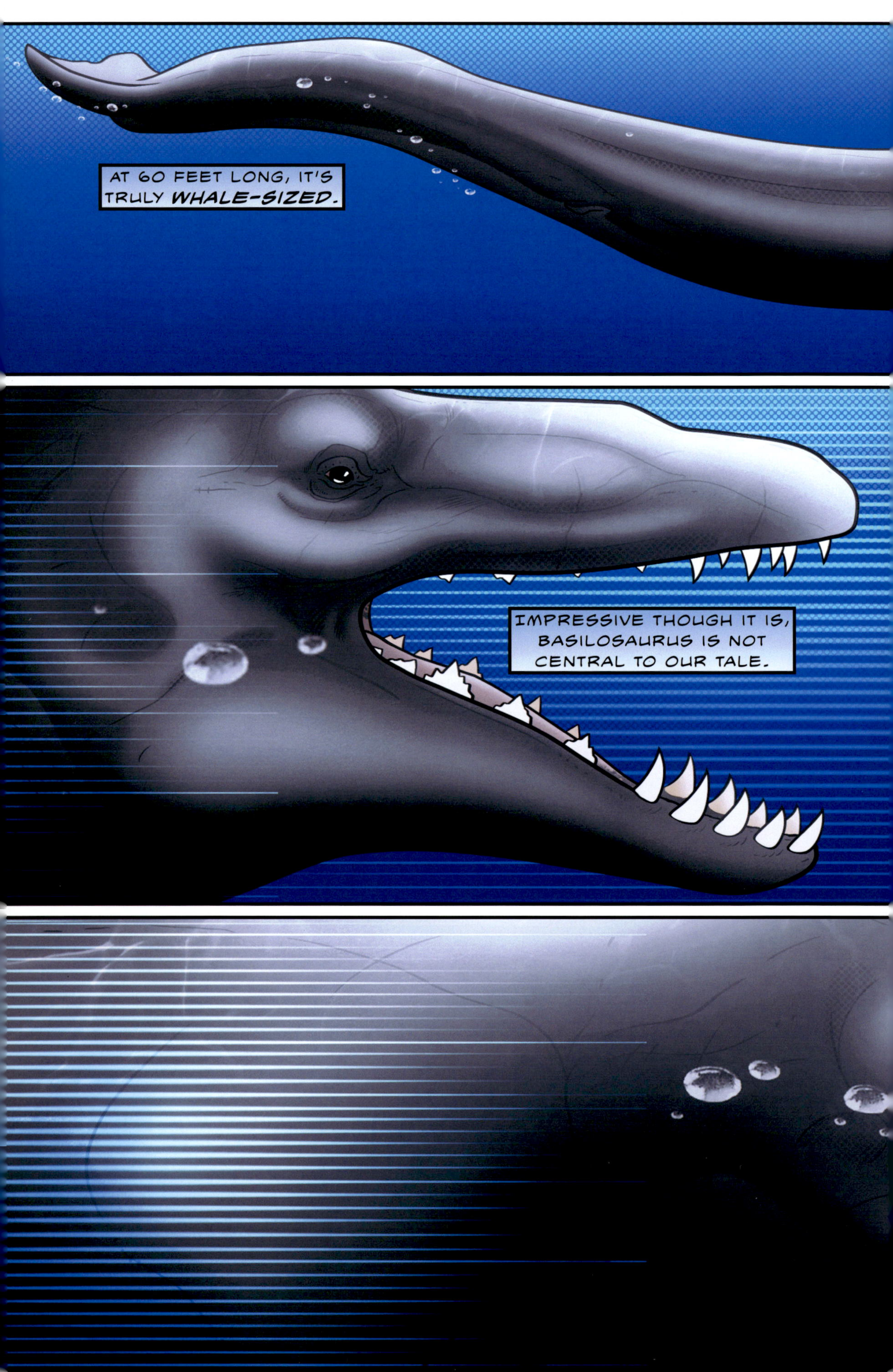

AT 60 FEET LONG, IT'S TRULY WHALE-SIZED.
IMPRESSIVE THOUGH IT IS, BASILOSAURUS IS NOT CENTRAL TO OUR TALE.

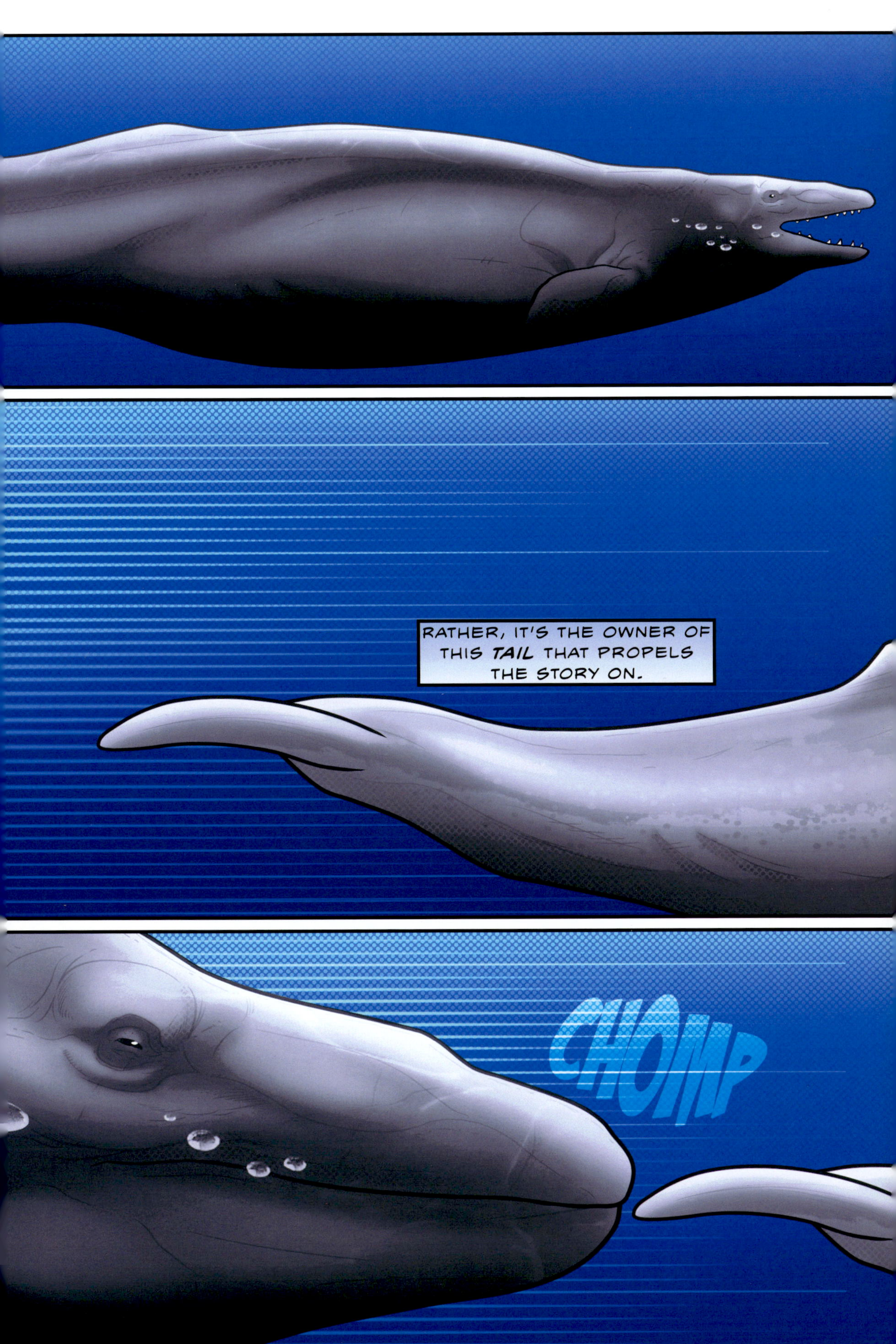

RATHER, IT'S THE OWNER OF THIS *TAIL* THAT PROPELS THE STORY ON.
CHOMP

BASILOSAURUS IS AN AMBUSH HUNTER.
IT'S NOT BUILT FOR SUSTAINED SPEED.

THIS YOUNG DORUDON IS JUST FAST ENOUGH TO OUT-SWIM THE FEROCIOUS PREDATOR –
AND REJOIN THE SAFETY OF ITS POD.

THE MIGHTY HUNTER IS SOMETHING OF AN EVOLUTIONARY DEAD END.

THE LONG, *SUPER-EEL* BODY TYPE DIED OUT WITH BASILOSAURUS.
MODERN WHALES WENT IN A DIFFERENT DIRECTION.

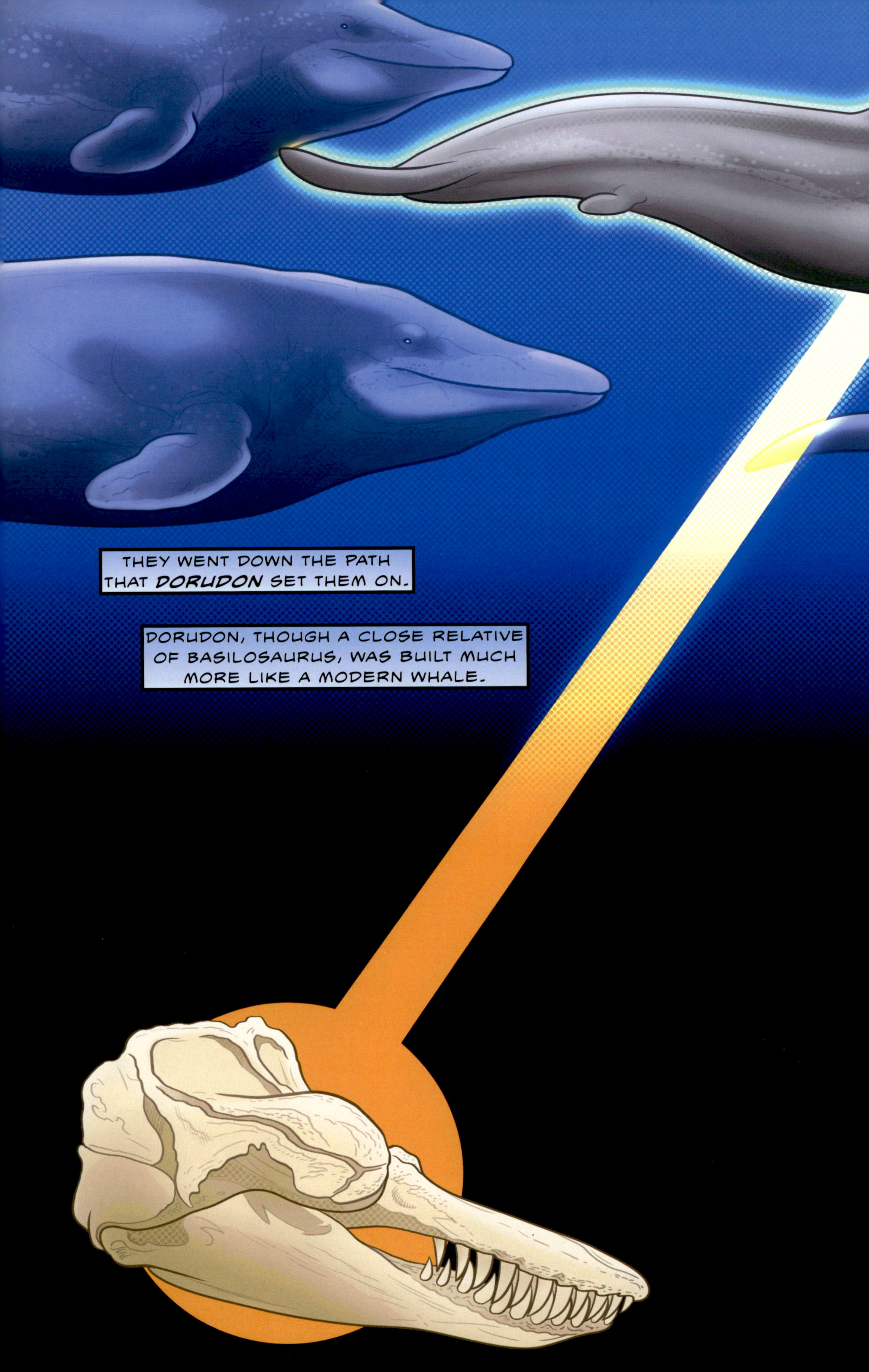

THEY WENT DOWN THE PATH THAT *DORUDON* SET THEM ON.
DORUDON, THOUGH A CLOSE RELATIVE OF BASILOSAURUS, WAS BUILT MUCH MORE LIKE A MODERN WHALE.

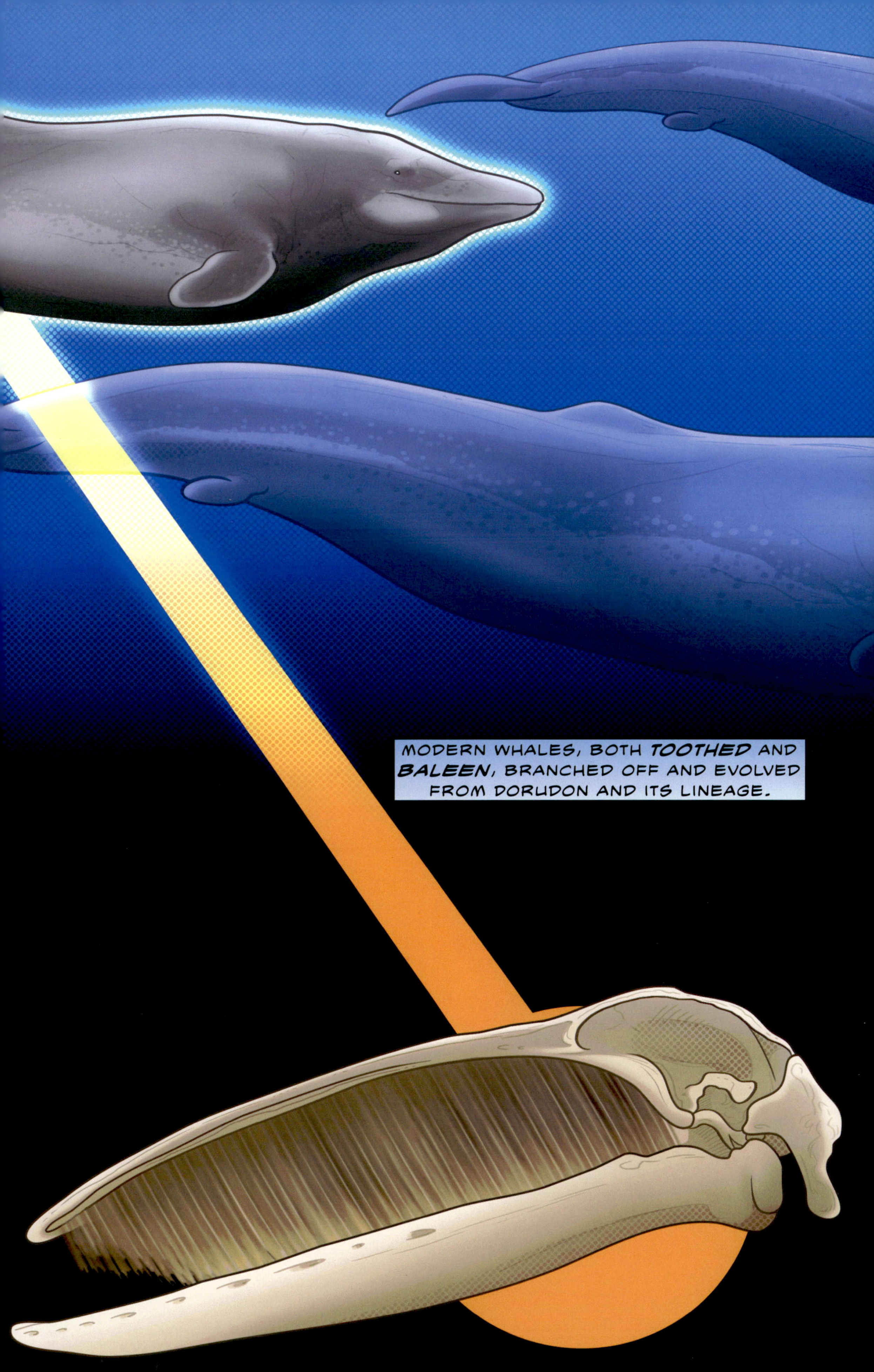

MODERN WHALES, BOTH *TOOTHED* AND *BALEEN*, BRANCHED OFF AND EVOLVED FROM DORUDON AND ITS LINEAGE.

15 MILLION YEARS AGO
THESE WHALES - CALLED CETOTHERIUM - LOOK MUCH LIKE MANY OF THE WHALES WE KNOW TODAY.
THOUGH NOT GIANTS - ONLY ABOUT 15 FEET LONG - THEY EMPLOY THE SAME FEEDING STRATEGY THAT THEIR TITANIC DESCENDANTS WILL USE IN THE FUTURE.
THE CETOTHERIUM TAKE BIG GULPS OF WATER -
THEN THEY PUSH IT ALL BACK OUT THROUGH THEIR BALEEN BRISTLES.
THE BALEEN FUNCTION AS GIANT FILTERS, CATCHING KRILL, PLANKTON, AND OTHER SMALL FRY.
IT MAY SEEM ODD THAT THESE LARGE ANIMALS GET BY EATING THE SMALLEST FOODS -

BUT IT
WORKS.

SINCE THE FIRST OF THEIR LINE - PAKICETUS - WHALES HAVE BEEN PREDATORS -
HUNTING DOWN AND EATING ANYTHING THEY COULD GET THEIR TEETH ON.
AND, WHILE THESE WHALES ARE TECHNICALLY PREYING ON TINY SEA CREATURES -

HERE, IN THE MIOCENE OCEAN, THERE ARE PREDATORS OF A MORE...TRADITIONAL FARE.

MEGALODON.
50 FEET LONG, AND WEIGHING MORE THAN 60 TONS -
IT'S THE BIGGEST SHARK.
EVER.

MEGALODON HAS THE STRONGEST BITE OF ANY ANIMAL —

STRONG ENOUGH TO BITE A WHALE IN HALF.

THIS MONSTER RULES THE SEAS UNCHALLENGED.

OR DOES IT?
THERE'S ANOTHER GIANT IN THE MIOCENE OCEAN —

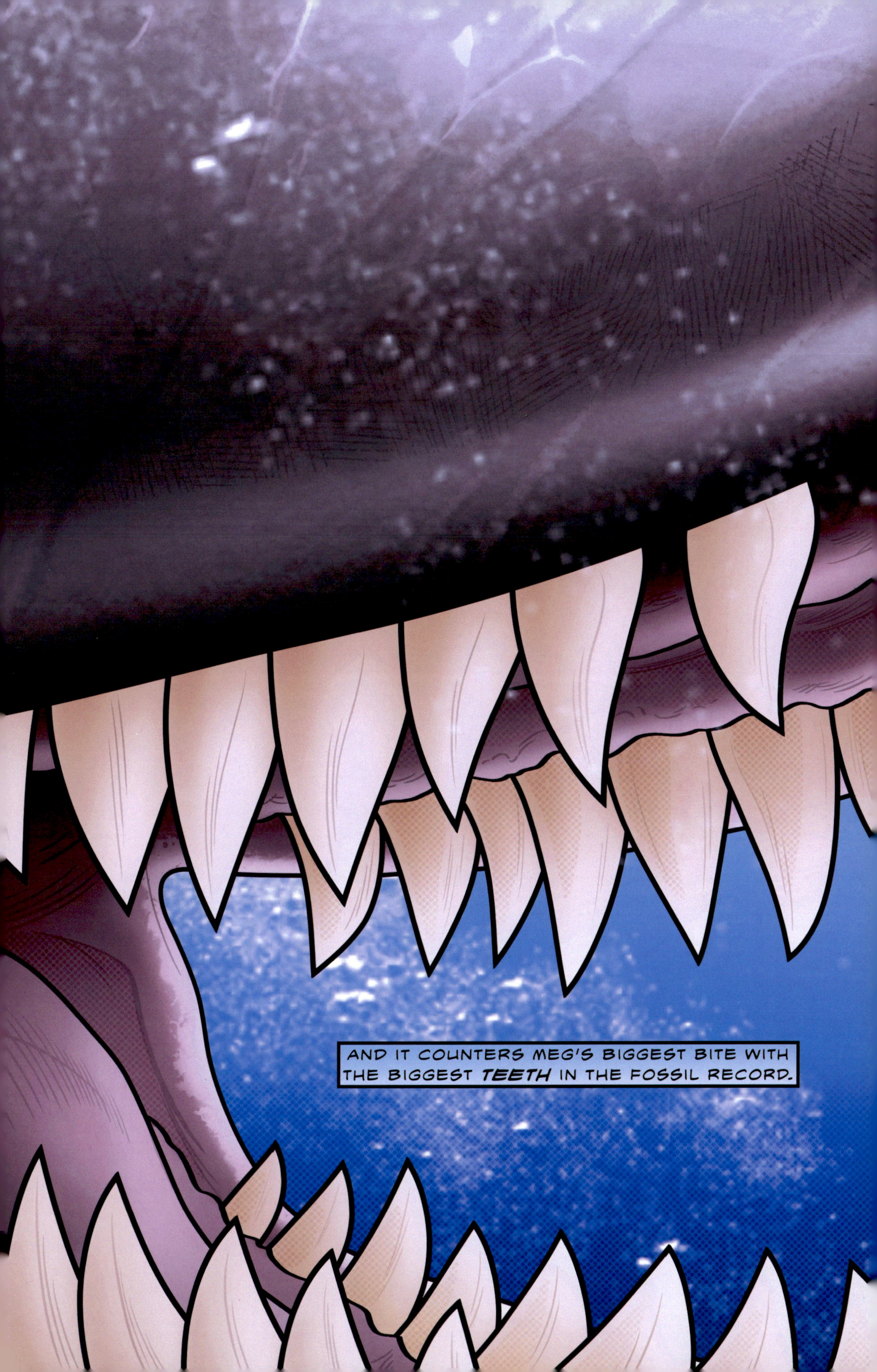
AND IT COUNTERS MEG'S BIGGEST BITE WITH THE BIGGEST *TEETH* IN THE FOSSIL RECORD.

LIVYATAN.
THIS SPERM WHALE MATCHES THE COLOSSAL MEGALODON IN SIZE.
UNLIKE ITS MODERN COUSINS WHO HUNT SQUID IN THE DARK OCEAN DEPTHS –
THIS WHALE USES ITS ENORMOUS TEETH TO HUNT LARGE PREY ON THE SURFACE.

IT'S A BEAST THAT SEEMS LIKE IT SHOULD BELONG TO THE REALM OF *MYTH.*
BUT HERE, IN THESE ANCIENT SEAS –
THE *LEVIATHAN* IS VERY *REAL.*

THOUGH IT'S A WHALE, LIVYATAN HAS NO LOYALTY TO ITS MAMMALIAN COUSINS.
THIS BEAST IS A WHALE-EATER.
WHAM

AND THAT PUTS IT IN DIRECT COMPETITION WITH THE MASSIVE SHARK.

MEGALODON AND LIVYATAN RULED THE MIOCENE SEAS.
AND WITH THESE TWO CHOMPING THEIR WAY THROUGH THE BLUE —
NOTHING WAS SAFE —

NOT EVEN EACH OTHER.

WHALES HAVE A LONG HISTORY OF BEING BIG.

BUT IT WASN'T UNTIL RECENTLY
- GEOLOGICALLY SPEAKING -
THAT THEY REALLY STARTED
TO PACK ON THE POUNDS.

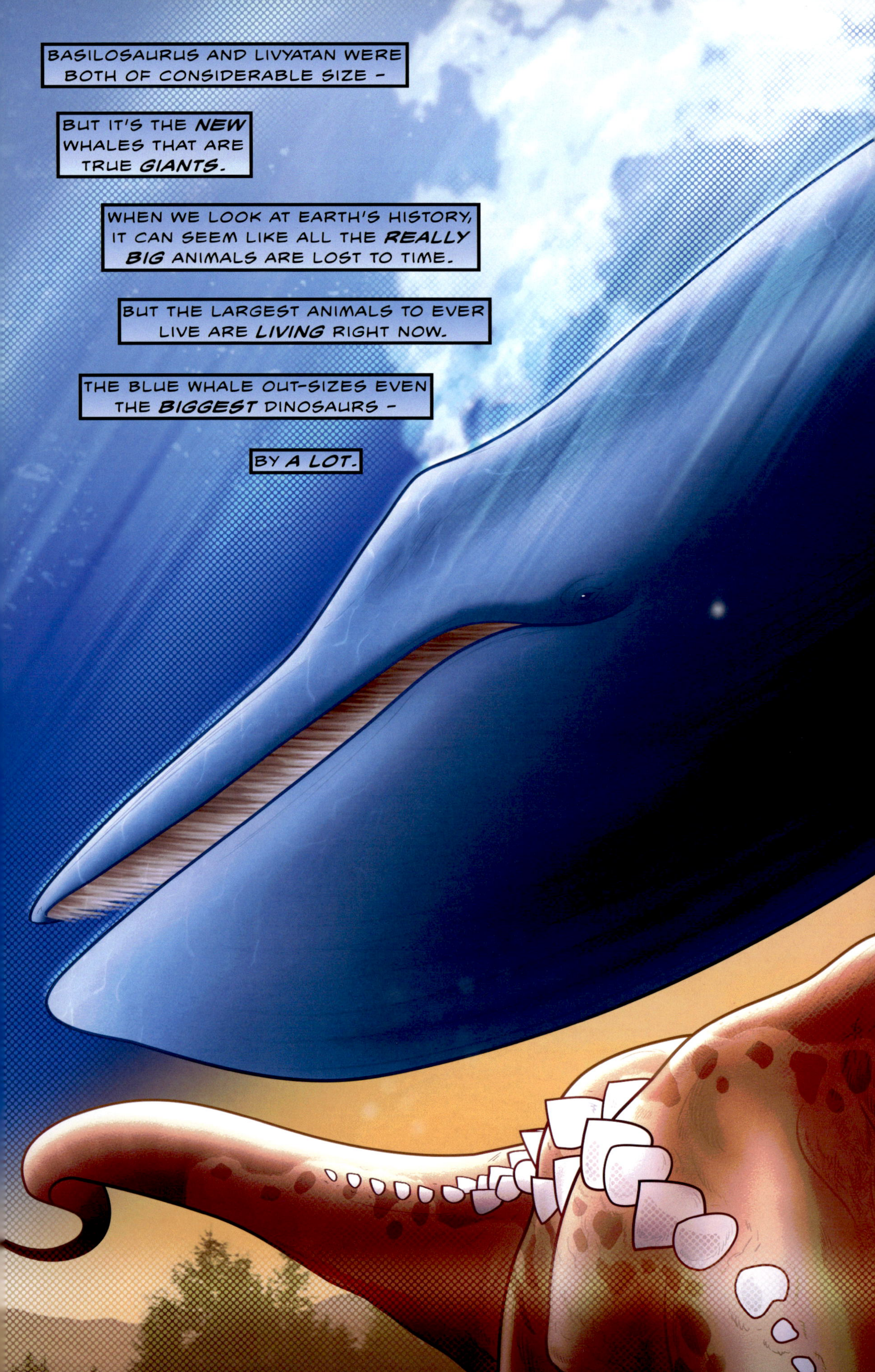

BASILOSAURUS AND LIVYATAN WERE BOTH OF CONSIDERABLE SIZE –
BUT IT'S THE *NEW* WHALES THAT ARE TRUE *GIANTS.*
WHEN WE LOOK AT EARTH'S HISTORY, IT CAN SEEM LIKE ALL THE *REALLY BIG* ANIMALS ARE LOST TO TIME.
BUT THE LARGEST ANIMALS TO EVER LIVE ARE *LIVING* RIGHT NOW.
THE BLUE WHALE OUT-SIZES EVEN THE *BIGGEST* DINOSAURS –
BY *A LOT.*

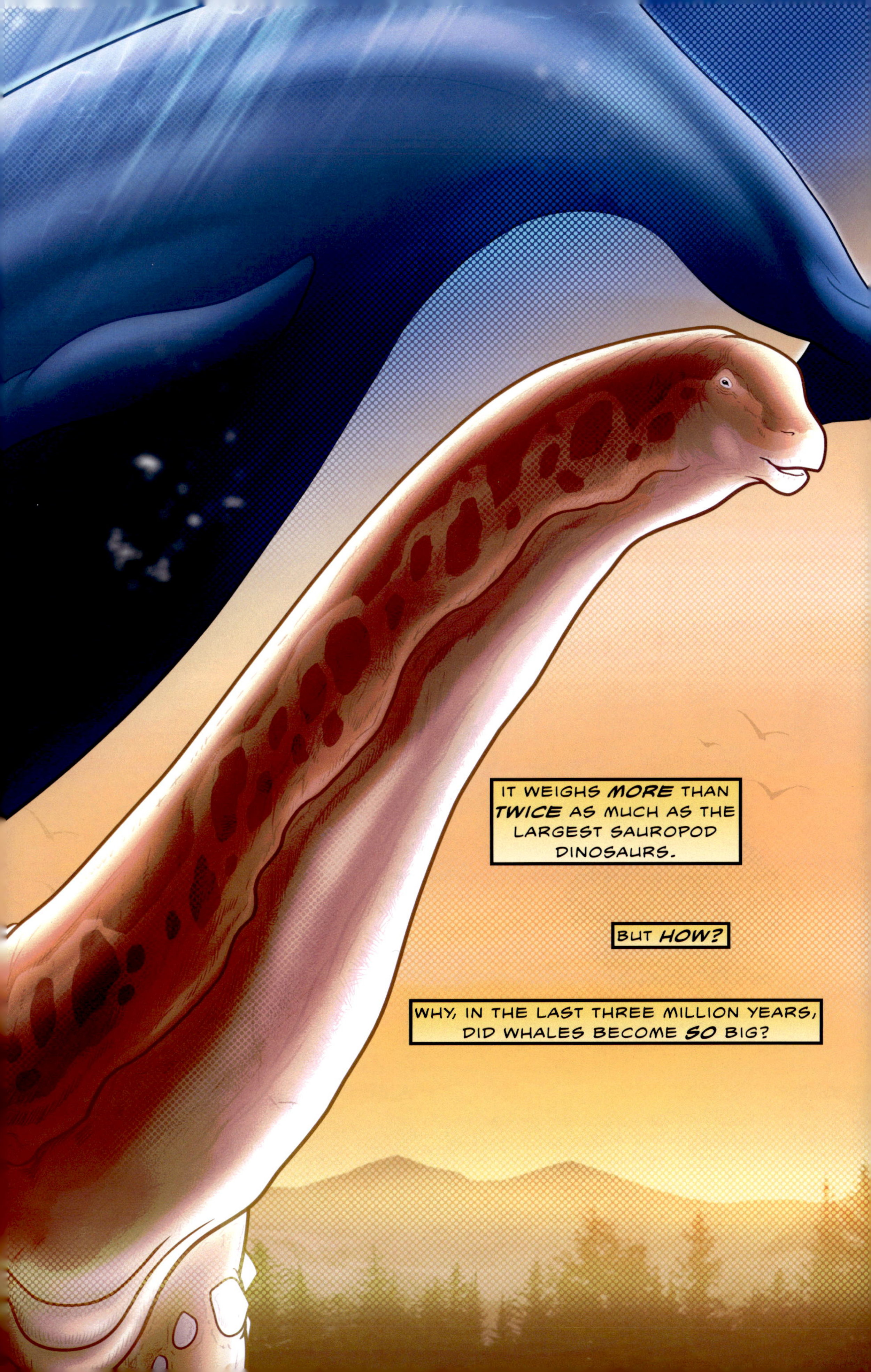

IT WEIGHS MORE THAN TWICE AS MUCH AS THE LARGEST SAUROPOD DINOSAURS.

BUT HOW?

WHY, IN THE LAST THREE MILLION YEARS, DID WHALES BECOME SO BIG?

THE ANSWER BEGINS WITH THE ICE AGE.
THE ICE SHEETS WERE SO LARGE THAT THEY GENERATED THEIR OWN WEATHER PATTERNS, CHANGING THE PLANET'S CLIMATE -

DURING THE PLEISTOCENE EPOCH - THE TIME OF MAMMOTHS AND SABER-CATS - VAST MOUNTAIN RANGES OF ICE - GLACIAL SHEETS - GREW ACROSS THE WORLD'S NORTHERN HEMISPHERE.

CREATING NEW SEASONAL CHANGES AND FLUCTUATIONS IN GLOBAL TEMPERATURE.

THE CHANGING CLIMATE AFFECTED THE OCEANS TOO.
STRONG WINDS ALTERED OCEAN CURRENTS —

BRINGING NUTRIENT-RICH WATERS FROM THE DEEP OCEANS UP TO THE SURFACE.
WHEN THE ICE AGE FINALLY GAVE WAY, THE WATER FROM MELTING ICE SHEETS ENDED UP IN THE OCEANS, ADDING EVEN MORE NUTRIENTS TO THE MIX.
THESE BOUNTIFUL WATERS ATTRACTED SMALL FISH, PLANKTON, AND KRILL - WHOSE POPULATIONS BOOMED.

BUT IT WASN'T SO *SIMPLE.* THOUGH THERE WERE GIANT *SMORGASBORDS* OF WHALE FOOD, OCEAN CURRENTS CONCENTRATED THEM OFF IN REMOTE AREAS, DISTANT FROM ONE ANOTHER.

AND BIGGER ANIMALS CAN COVER GREATER DISTANCE MORE EFFICIENTLY THAN SMALL ONES.

ALL THAT IS TO SAY: MORE FOOD + LONG DISTANCE TRAVEL = *BIGGER WHALES.*

THE BLUE WHALE IS THE LARGEST ANIMAL TO EVER ROAM THE EARTH —
CRUISING THE SEAS, ON THE SEARCH FOR KRILL.
AT NEARLY 200 TONS, THE BLUE WHALE FACES ALMOST NO NATURAL THREAT.

OCEANS ARE HOME TO CREATURES BIG AND SMALL.
GENTLE GIANTS AND VORACIOUS PREDATORS ALIKE SHARE THE SEAS.

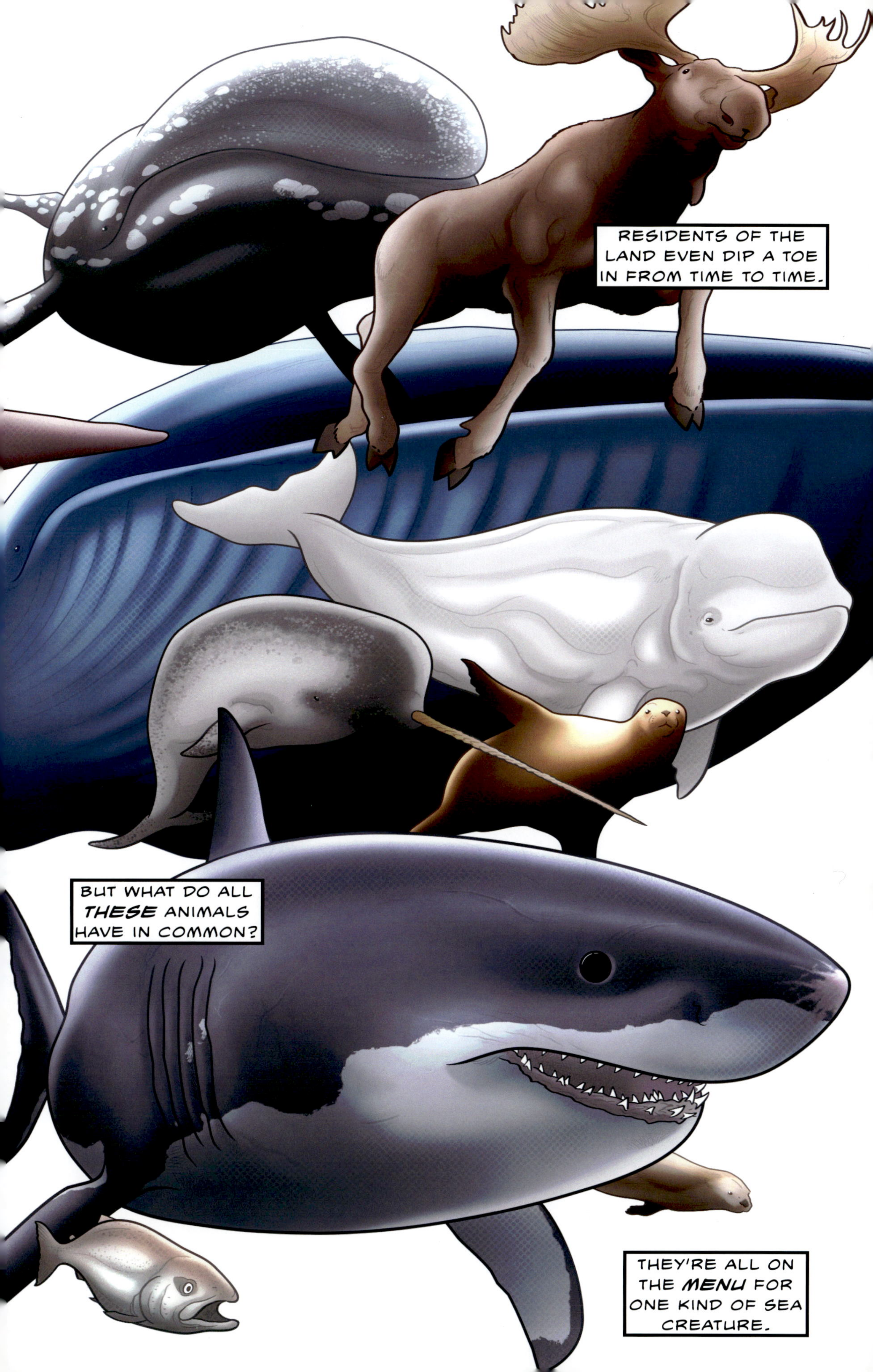

RESIDENTS OF THE LAND EVEN DIP A TOE IN FROM TIME TO TIME.
BUT WHAT DO ALL *THESE* ANIMALS HAVE IN COMMON?
THEY'RE ALL ON THE *MENU* FOR ONE KIND OF SEA CREATURE.

ORCAS.
PERHAPS - WITH THE EXCEPTION OF HUMANITY - THE GREATEST PREDATORS THE PLANET HAS EVER SEEN.
FEMALES GROW TO 20 FEET LONG AND CAN WEIGH 4 TONS.
MALES CAN MEASURE MORE THAN 25 FEET LONG, AND WEIGH OVER 6 TONS.

THESE HUNTERS CAN REACH SPEEDS OF MORE THAN 30 KNOTS - THAT'S ABOUT 34 MILES PER HOUR FOR YOU LANDLUBBERS.
AND THEY'RE SMART.
SCARY SMART.
AND THEY HUNT IN PACKS.

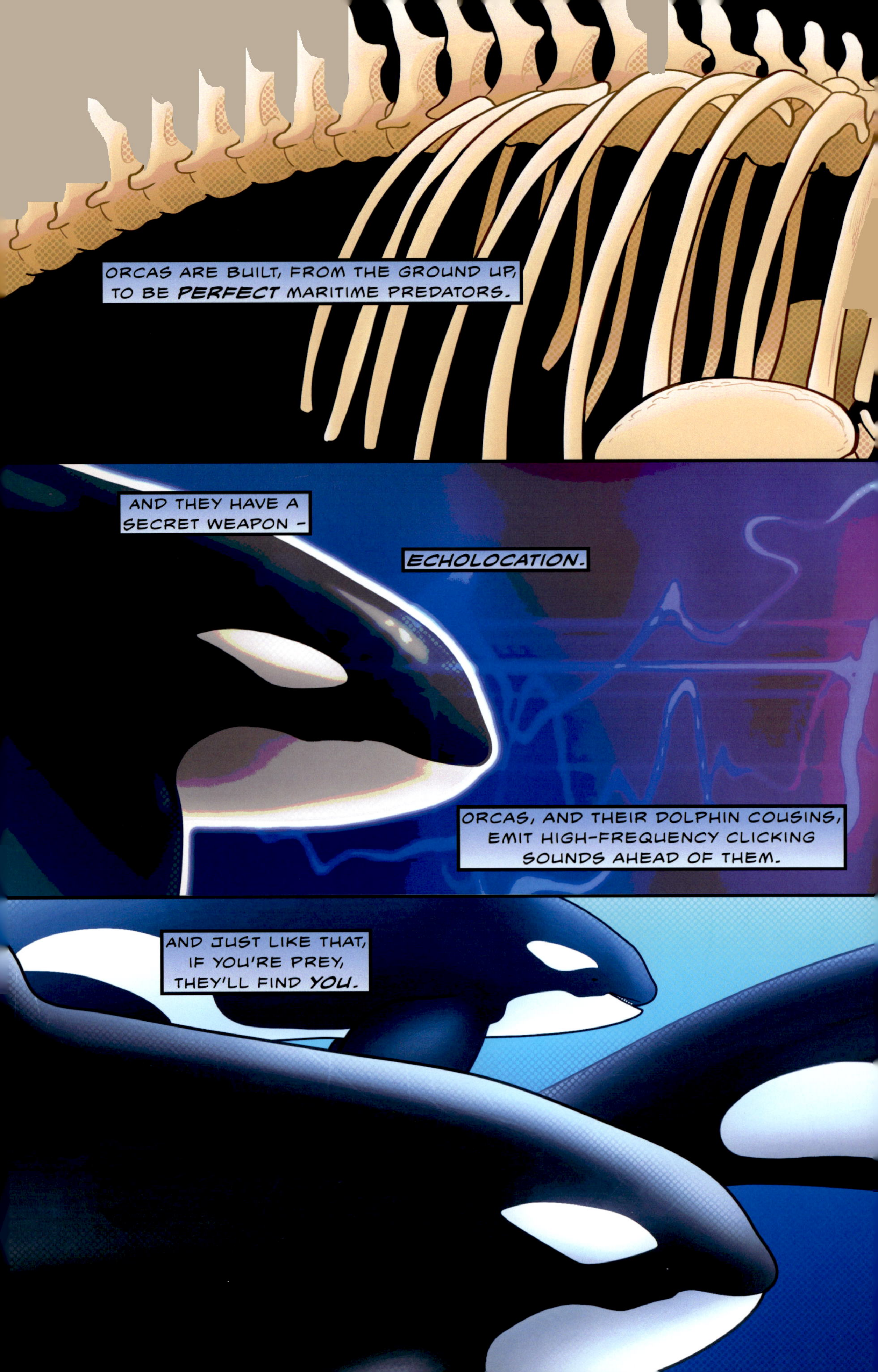

ORCAS ARE BUILT, FROM THE GROUND UP, TO BE PERFECT MARITIME PREDATORS.
AND THEY HAVE A SECRET WEAPON –
ECHOLOCATION.
ORCAS, AND THEIR DOLPHIN COUSINS, EMIT HIGH-FREQUENCY CLICKING SOUNDS AHEAD OF THEM.
AND JUST LIKE THAT, IF YOU'RE PREY, THEY'LL FIND YOU.

WITH DENTITION THAT WOULD IMPRESS A T. REX, ONCE THEY GRAB SOMETHING —
IT'S NOT GETTING AWAY.
WHEN THOSE SOUNDS REACH A PREY ANIMAL — SAY, A FISH, MAYBE A SEAL, OR, OH, I DON'T KNOW, A GREAT WHITE SHARK — THEY BOUNCE BACK AND ARE PICKED UP BY SPECIAL SENSORS ON THE ORCA'S FACE AND HEAD.
EDITOR'S NOTE: NO NEED TO ACTUALLY WORRY — ORCAS DON'T ATTACK PEOPLE. PHEW!

ORCAS, OFTEN CALLED KILLER WHALES, HAVE ANOTHER NICKNAME.

IT COMES FROM THEIR PACK-HUNTING, AND *RELENTLESS* PURSUIT OF PREY.

WOLVES OF THE SEA.

ORCAS HOLD SIGNIFICANCE IN MANY CULTURES AROUND THE WORLD, PARTICULARLY WITH THOSE OF NATIVE AMERICANS AND FIRST NATIONS PEOPLES OF THE PACIFIC NORTHWEST.
THESE FIRST PEOPLE ON THE NORTH AMERICAN CONTINENT HOLD THE WHALES IN HIGH REGARD.

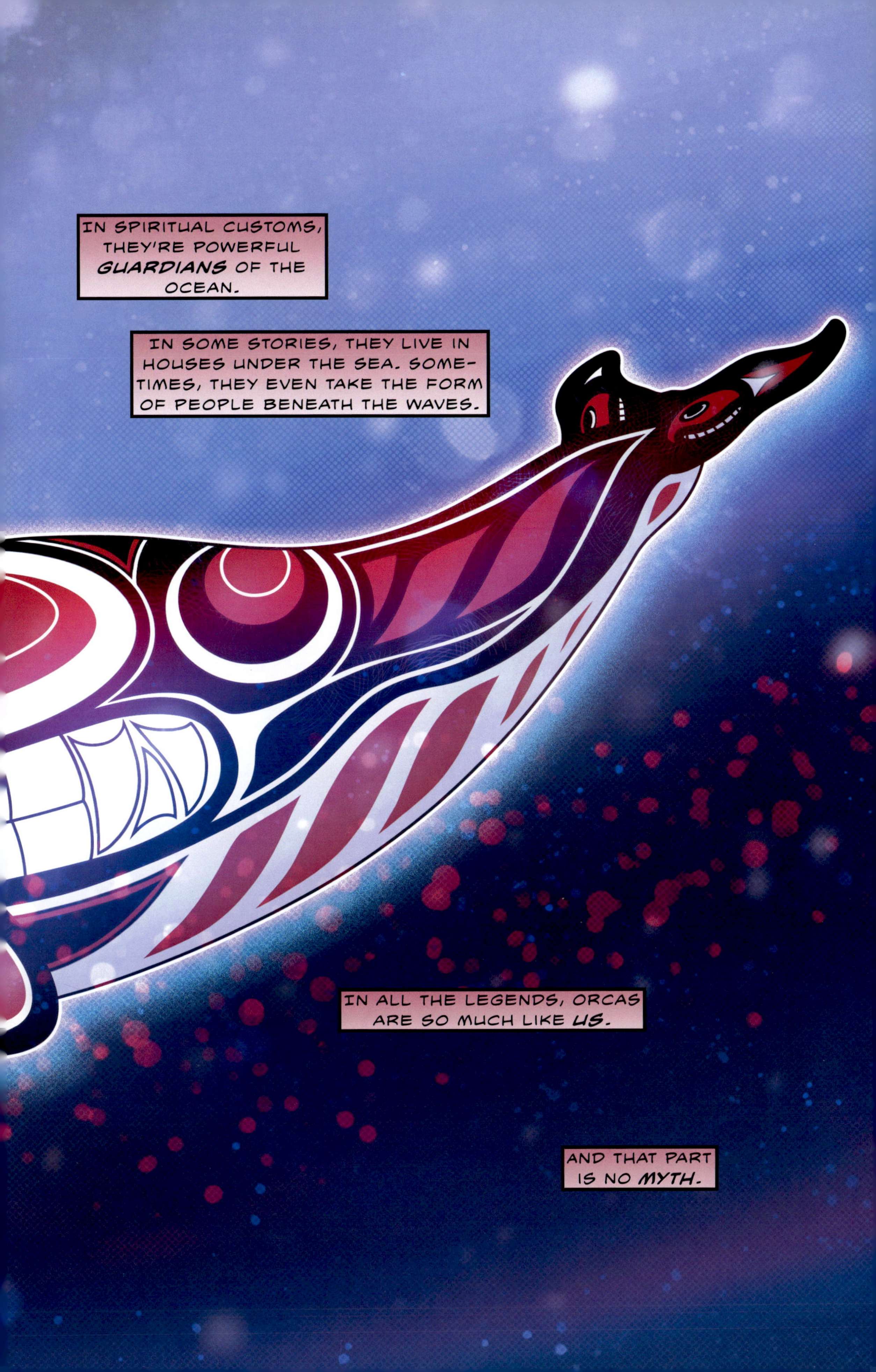

IN SPIRITUAL CUSTOMS, THEY'RE POWERFUL *GUARDIANS* OF THE OCEAN.

IN SOME STORIES, THEY LIVE IN HOUSES UNDER THE SEA. SOMETIMES, THEY EVEN TAKE THE FORM OF PEOPLE BENEATH THE WAVES.

IN ALL THE LEGENDS, ORCAS ARE SO MUCH LIKE *US.*

AND THAT PART IS NO *MYTH.*

ORCAS ARE CURIOUS AND CARING.

LIKE ALL WHALES, THEY ARE THINKING, SENTIENT BEINGS.

LIKE US, THEY HAVE A PROFOUND *LOVE* FOR THEIR YOUNG.
AND THEY STAY WITH THEIR FAMILIES FOR THEIR ENTIRE LIVES.
WITH A LIFESPAN THAT CAN LAST A *CENTURY*, THOSE ARE STRONG BONDS.
ORCAS - *LIKE US* - ARE MORE THAN JUST FEROCIOUS PREDATORS.

ORCAS LIVE IN EVERY OCEAN ON EARTH.

AND, JUST LIKE PEOPLE WHO LIVE ALL OVER THE WORLD –
THEY HAVE DIFFERENT LANGUAGES AND CULTURES.
ORCAS ARE INTELLIGENT, STRONG, SOCIAL, AND YES – FEARSOME.

BUT THEY ARE NOT UNRIVALED.
ONE SMACK FROM THIS TAIL —

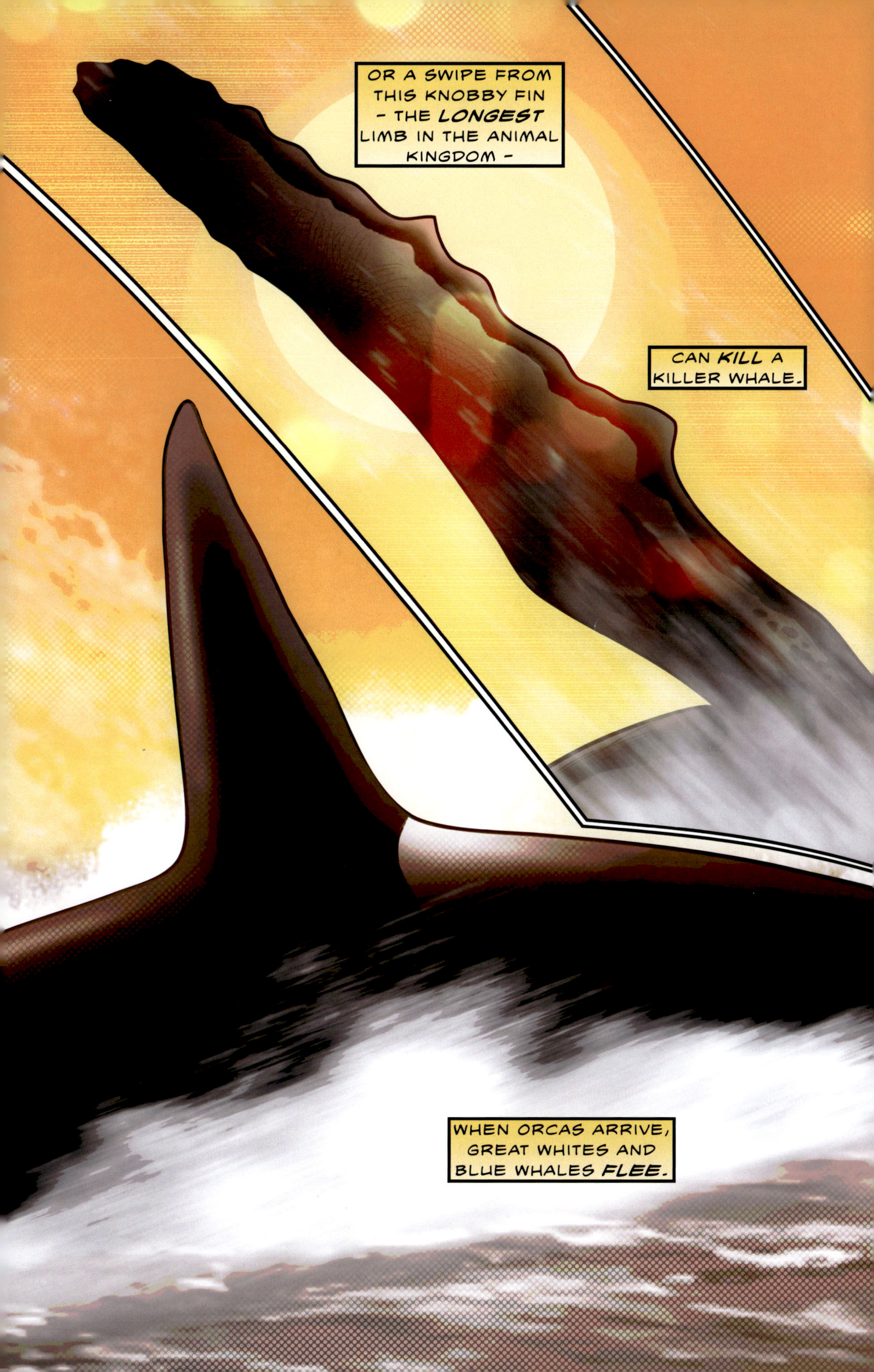

OR A SWIPE FROM THIS KNOBBY FIN - THE LONGEST LIMB IN THE ANIMAL KINGDOM -
CAN KILL A KILLER WHALE.
WHEN ORCAS ARRIVE, GREAT WHITES AND BLUE WHALES FLEE.

HUMPBACKS DO NOT.

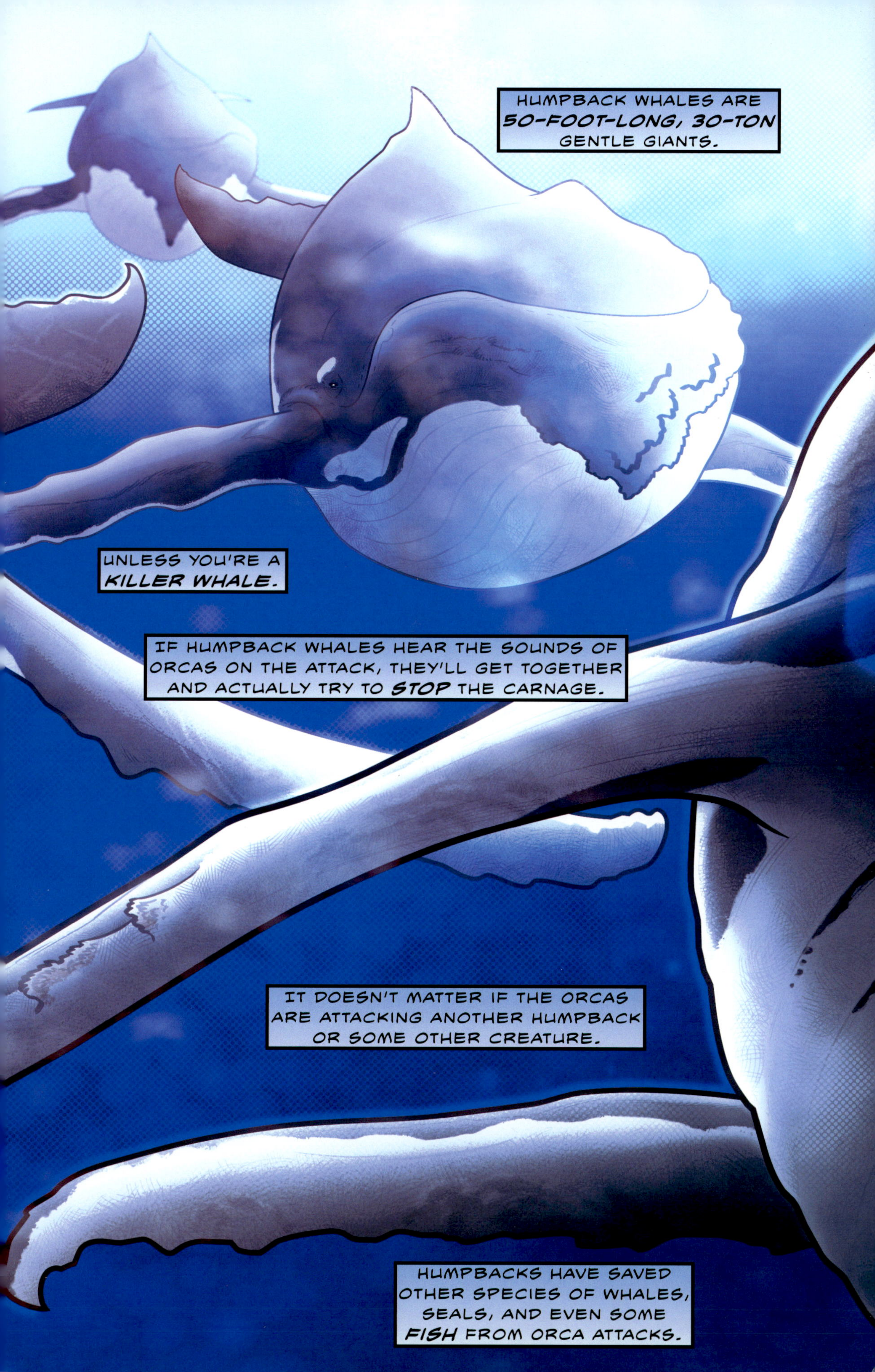

HUMPBACK WHALES ARE 50-FOOT-LONG, 30-TON GENTLE GIANTS.
UNLESS YOU'RE A KILLER WHALE.
IF HUMPBACK WHALES HEAR THE SOUNDS OF ORCAS ON THE ATTACK, THEY'LL GET TOGETHER AND ACTUALLY TRY TO STOP THE CARNAGE.
IT DOESN'T MATTER IF THE ORCAS ARE ATTACKING ANOTHER HUMPBACK OR SOME OTHER CREATURE.
HUMPBACKS HAVE SAVED OTHER SPECIES OF WHALES, SEALS, AND EVEN SOME FISH FROM ORCA ATTACKS.

MANY ADULT HUMPBACKS ARE SCARRED,
PHYSICALLY AND EMOTIONALLY,
FROM ENCOUNTERS WITH ORCAS.

BUT THAT'S EXACTLY WHY THEY RISK FIGHTING THE MOST POWERFUL PREDATOR THE SEAS HAVE EVER SEEN.
ORCAS WILL ATTACK AND KILL YOUNG HUMPBACKS AND *CALVES* IF GIVEN THE CHANCE.
AND SO, HUMPBACKS RESPOND WITH *FORCE*.
HUMPBACKS ARE *BIG*.
WITH *BARNACLE-COVERED* FINS THAT ACT LIKE GIANT BRASS KNUCKLES, THEY'RE *WELL-ARMED*.
EVEN THE *WOLVES OF THE SEA* GIVE HUMPBACKS *RESPECT*.

AS LONG AS YOU'RE NOT AN ORCA, HUMPBACKS ARE KNOWN TO BE QUITE FRIENDLY.
THEY INTERACT WITH OTHER SPECIES PEACEFULLY.
LIKE ALL WHALES, THEY'RE HIGHLY INTELLIGENT.

HUMPBACKS' SAVING OF OTHER ANIMALS HAS RAISED DISCUSSION ABOUT THE CONCEPT OF *ANIMAL-ALTRUISM.* IT DOESN'T APPEAR THAT SAVING OTHER SPECIES FROM BEING KILLED BY ORCAS HELPS THE *HUMPBACKS* IN ANY WAY.

YET THEY STILL DO IT.

IT'S BEEN SUGGESTED THAT HUMPBACKS HAVE EVEN *SHIELDED* HUMAN DIVERS FROM *SHARK-ATTACK.*

IT SEEMS THEIR *KINDNESS* EXTENDS EVEN TO *US.*

THOUGH, IT WOULD BE UNDERSTANDABLE IF THAT WERE *NOT* THE CASE.

WHALING - HUMANS HUNTING WHALES - HAS BEEN GOING ON FOR THOUSANDS OF YEARS.
MEAT FROM A WHALE-HUNT COULD FEED A WHOLE COMMUNITY THROUGH A LONG, COLD WINTER.
THIS PRACTICE IS CALLED SUBSISTENCE HUNTING.
BUT BY THE 16TH CENTURY, DRIVEN BY HIGH DEMAND FOR WHALE OIL FROM EUROPEAN NATIONS, WHALING HAD BECOME AN INDUSTRY.
WHALE OIL - RENDERED FROM A DEAD WHALE'S BLUBBER - WAS WELL SUITED TO FUEL LANTERNS THROUGHOUT EARLY INDUSTRIAL SOCIETY.
IT LUBRICATED THE MACHINES THAT POWERED THE INDUSTRIAL REVOLUTION.

AND SO, IN THE NAME OF ECONOMIC PROGRESS, WHALES BECAME A TARGET.
KILLING AS COMMERCE HAD BEGUN.
BY THE MID 1800'S, IN THE AMERICAN NORTHEAST, NEW ENGLAND WAS THE WHALING CAPITAL OF THE WORLD.
HUNDREDS OF SHIPS - AND THOUSANDS OF MEN - POURED OUT OF PLACES LIKE NANTUCKET AND CAPE COD.
THEY SAILED TO THE FAR CORNERS OF THE WORLD, ALWAYS ON THE HUNT.

SOME WHALES FOUGHT BACK —

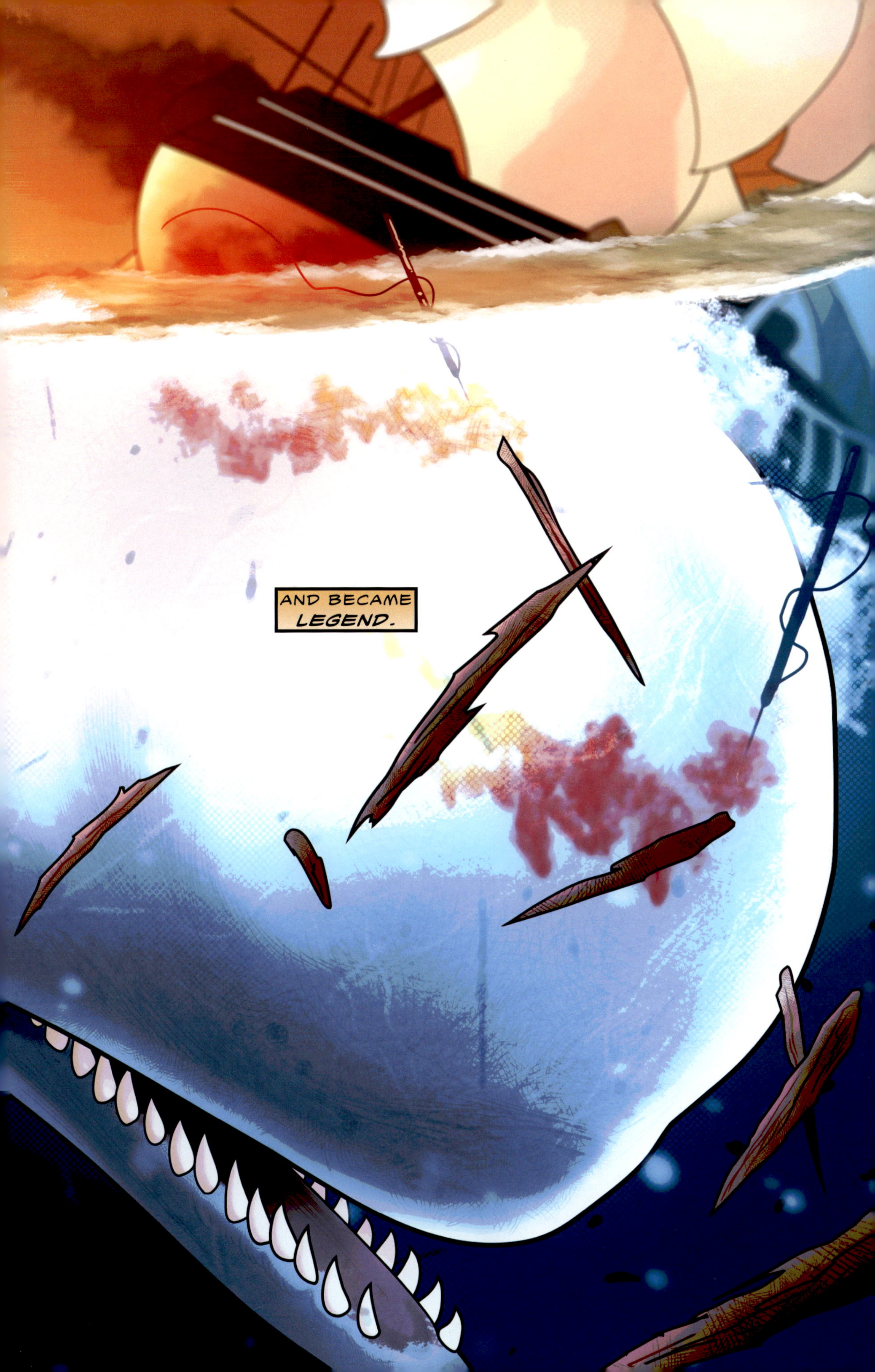
AND BECAME LEGEND.

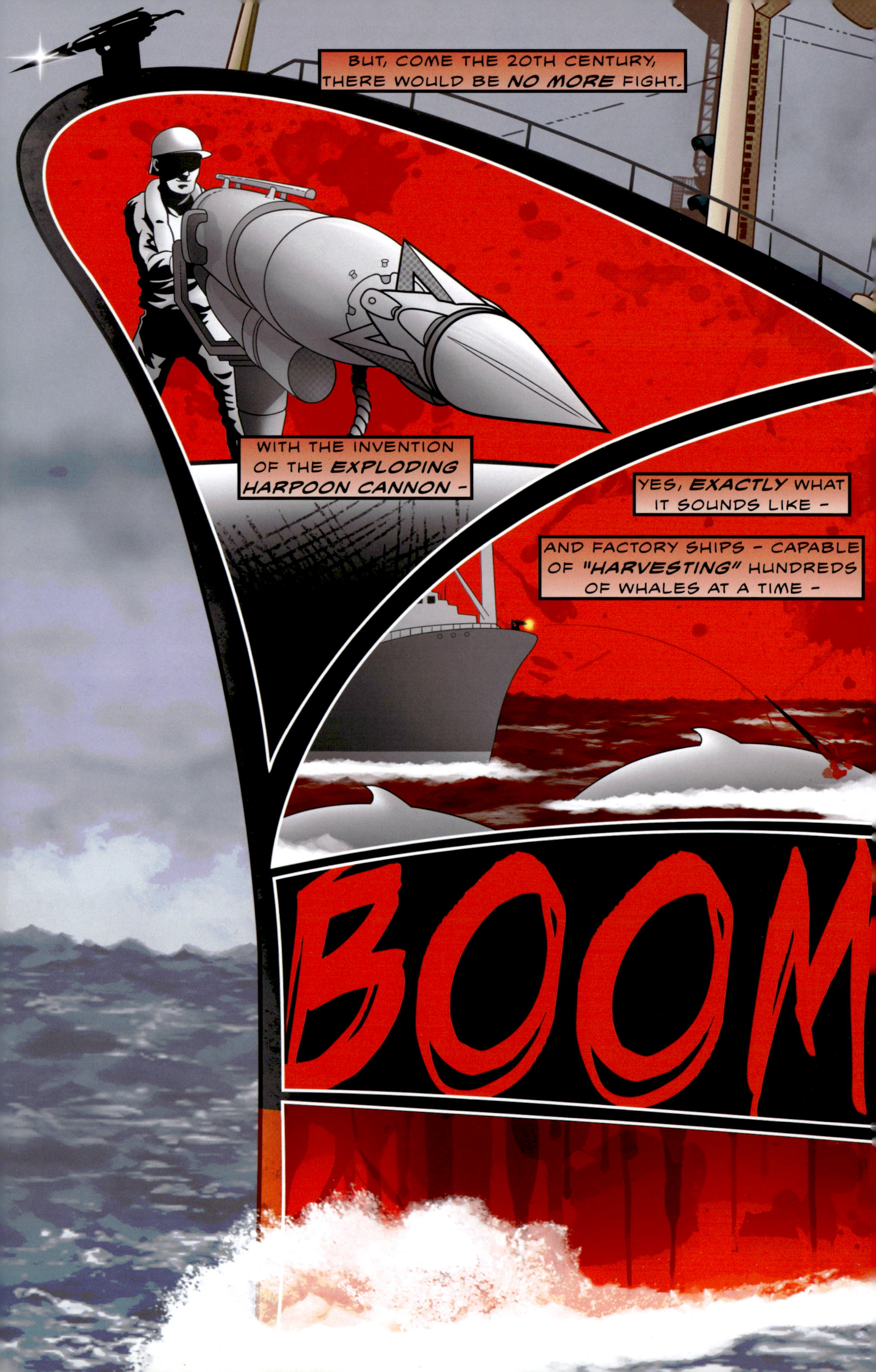

BUT, COME THE 20TH CENTURY, THERE WOULD BE NO MORE FIGHT.
WITH THE INVENTION OF THE EXPLODING HARPOON CANNON –
YES, EXACTLY WHAT IT SOUNDS LIKE –
AND FACTORY SHIPS – CAPABLE OF "HARVESTING" HUNDREDS OF WHALES AT A TIME –
BOOM

THERE COULD BE NO MORE FIGHT.
BY THE 1930'S, MORE THAN 50,000 WHALES WERE SLAUGHTERED EVERY YEAR.
FIFTY MILLION YEARS OF EVOLUTION, BROUGHT TO THE VERY BRINK OF EXTINCTION IN THE GEOLOGIC BLINK OF AN EYE.

AND IT'S NOT JUST ACTIVE KILLING THAT'S A THREAT.
FOR YEARS, WORLD MILITARIES HAVE BEEN WAGING INCIDENTAL WAR AGAINST WHALE POPULATIONS.

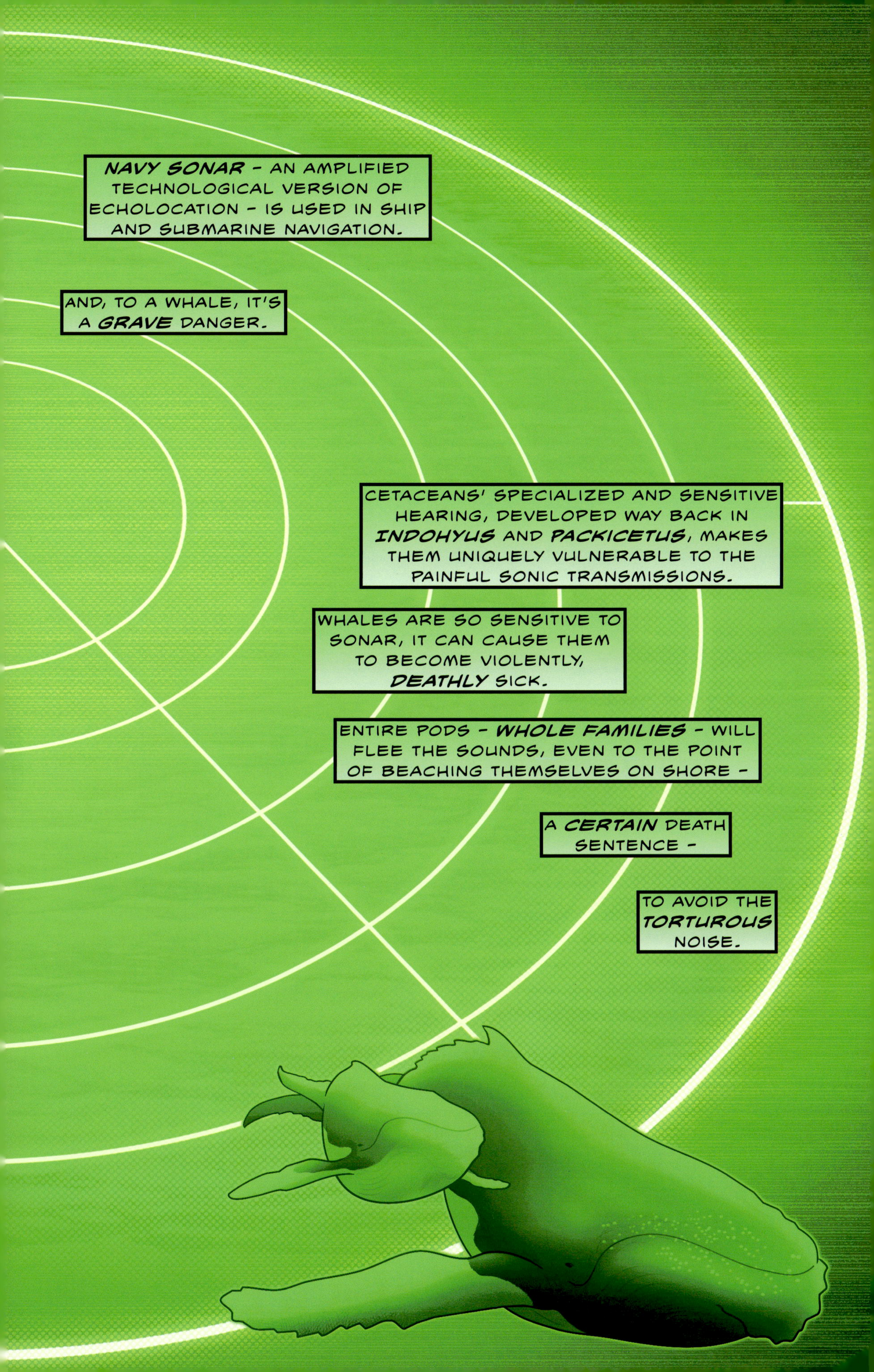

NAVY SONAR – AN AMPLIFIED TECHNOLOGICAL VERSION OF ECHOLOCATION – IS USED IN SHIP AND SUBMARINE NAVIGATION.

AND, TO A WHALE, IT'S A *GRAVE* DANGER.

CETACEANS' SPECIALIZED AND SENSITIVE HEARING, DEVELOPED WAY BACK IN *INDOHYUS* AND *PACKICETUS*, MAKES THEM UNIQUELY VULNERABLE TO THE PAINFUL SONIC TRANSMISSIONS.

WHALES ARE SO SENSITIVE TO SONAR, IT CAN CAUSE THEM TO BECOME VIOLENTLY, *DEATHLY* SICK.

ENTIRE PODS – *WHOLE FAMILIES* – WILL FLEE THE SOUNDS, EVEN TO THE POINT OF BEACHING THEMSELVES ON SHORE –

A *CERTAIN* DEATH SENTENCE –

TO AVOID THE *TORTUROUS* NOISE.

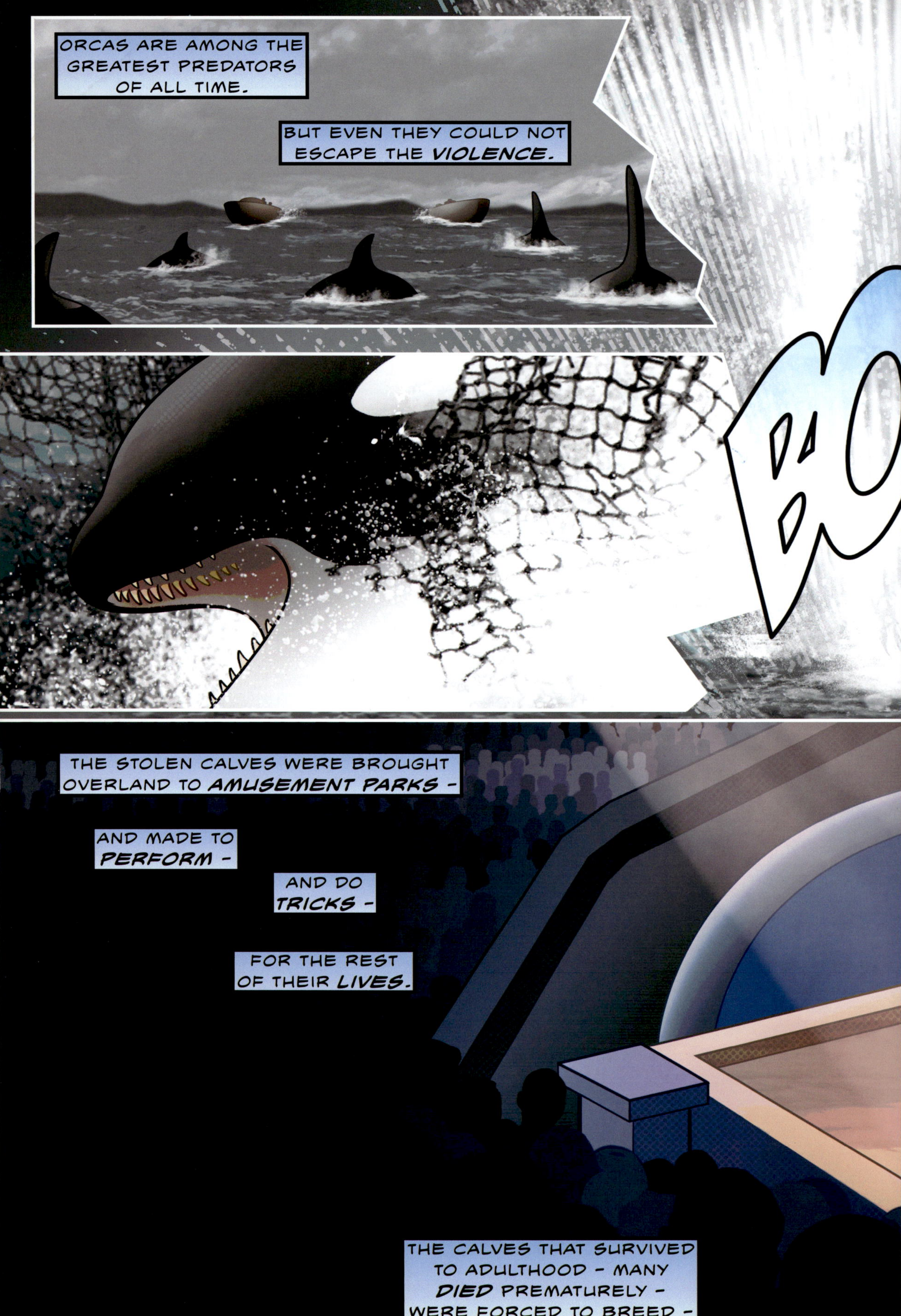

ORCAS ARE AMONG THE GREATEST PREDATORS OF ALL TIME.
BUT EVEN THEY COULD NOT ESCAPE THE VIOLENCE.
BO
THE STOLEN CALVES WERE BROUGHT OVERLAND TO AMUSEMENT PARKS —
AND MADE TO PERFORM —
AND DO TRICKS —
FOR THE REST OF THEIR LIVES.
THE CALVES THAT SURVIVED TO ADULTHOOD — MANY DIED PREMATURELY — WERE FORCED TO BREED —

IN THE 1970'S, IN THE WATERS OFF THE PACIFIC NORTHWEST, ORCAS WERE CHASED WITH SPEEDBOATS AND EXPLOSIVES.
THEY WERE HERDED INTO NET CAGES.
BOOM
AND THERE, CALVES - CHILDREN - WERE TORN FROM THEIR MOTHERS AND FAMILIES -
NEVER TO SEE THE OPEN SEA AGAIN.
SO THAT THESE PARKS WOULD NEVER RUN OUT OF ENTERTAINMENT.

RECENTLY, THOUGH, THE TIDES HAVE BEGUN TO CHANGE.
PEOPLE STARTED WONDERING –
WHAT IS THE MORALITY OF KILLING OR IMPRISONING LIVING BEINGS WITH HIGH LEVELS OF INTELLIGENCE AND *EMOTION?*
IN 1986, THE WORLD COMMUNITY – WITH THE EXCEPTION OF A FEW *ROGUE NATIONS* – AGREED TO BAN COMMERCIAL WHALING.
IN THE DECADES SINCE, WHALE POPULATIONS – ONCE ON THE VERGE OF TOTAL *ANNIHILATION* – HAVE REBOUNDED.
AND *FINALLY*, IN 2016, SEA-THEMED AMUSEMENT PARKS – UNDER *INTENSE* PRESSURE FROM PUBLIC DEMAND – AGREED TO STOP BREEDING CAPTIVE ORCAS.

TODAY, WHALE-WATCHING IS A MULTI-BILLION DOLLAR INDUSTRY.
CAPTAIN NATE'S WHALE WATCH
"LET'S GO SEE SOME CETACEANS!"
ATLAS VIII

IT SEEMS WE'VE CAUGHT ON AT LAST.
WHALES SHOULD BE ALIVE AND WILD.
BUT WHALES HAVE A VALUE FAR GREATER THAN ANY DOLLAR AMOUNT.
NOW, MORE THAN EVER.

OUR PLANET IS IN THE MIDST OF A CLIMATE EMERGENCY.
CARBON DIOXIDE — OR CO2 — EMITTED AS A BYPRODUCT FROM OUR CARS, PLANES, POWER PLANTS, AND ALMOST EVERY ASPECT OF MODERN HUMAN SOCIETY, SURROUNDS THE EARTH —
BUT THAT'S NOTHING COMPARED TO ANOTHER WAY WHALES COMBAT CLIMATE CHANGE.
WHEREVER WHALES LIVE, THERE IS ALSO PHYTOPLANKTON —
MICROSCOPIC OCEAN PLANTS THAT CONTRIBUTE FIFTY PERCENT OF THE PLANET'S OXYGEN —
AND CAPTURE 37 BILLION TONS OF CO2 EVERY YEAR.
THE PHYTOPLANKTON FEED ON THE NITROGEN AND IRON THAT IS PLENTIFUL IN WHALE EXCREMENT.
MORE WHALES MEANS MORE PHYTOPLANKTON SCRUBBING OUR ATMOSPHERE CLEAN.

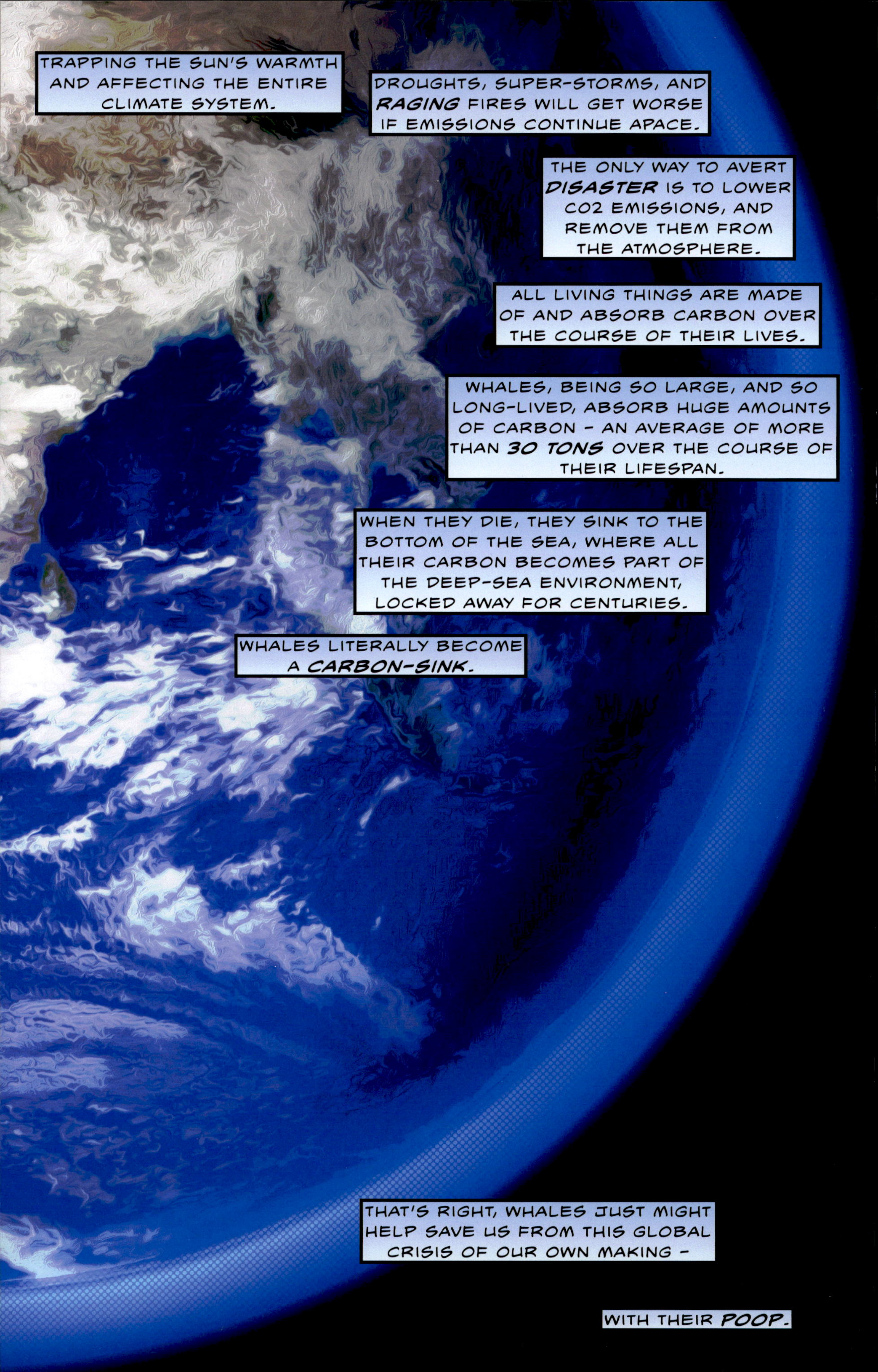

TRAPPING THE SUN'S WARMTH AND AFFECTING THE ENTIRE CLIMATE SYSTEM.

DROUGHTS, SUPER-STORMS, AND *RAGING* FIRES WILL GET WORSE IF EMISSIONS CONTINUE APACE.

THE ONLY WAY TO AVERT *DISASTER* IS TO LOWER CO2 EMISSIONS, AND REMOVE THEM FROM THE ATMOSPHERE.

ALL LIVING THINGS ARE MADE OF AND ABSORB CARBON OVER THE COURSE OF THEIR LIVES.

WHALES, BEING SO LARGE, AND SO LONG-LIVED, ABSORB HUGE AMOUNTS OF CARBON – AN AVERAGE OF MORE THAN *30 TONS* OVER THE COURSE OF THEIR LIFESPAN.

WHEN THEY DIE, THEY SINK TO THE BOTTOM OF THE SEA, WHERE ALL THEIR CARBON BECOMES PART OF THE DEEP-SEA ENVIRONMENT, LOCKED AWAY FOR CENTURIES.

WHALES LITERALLY BECOME A *CARBON-SINK*.

THAT'S RIGHT, WHALES JUST MIGHT HELP SAVE US FROM THIS GLOBAL CRISIS OF OUR OWN MAKING –

WITH THEIR *POOP*.

47 MILLION YEARS AGO

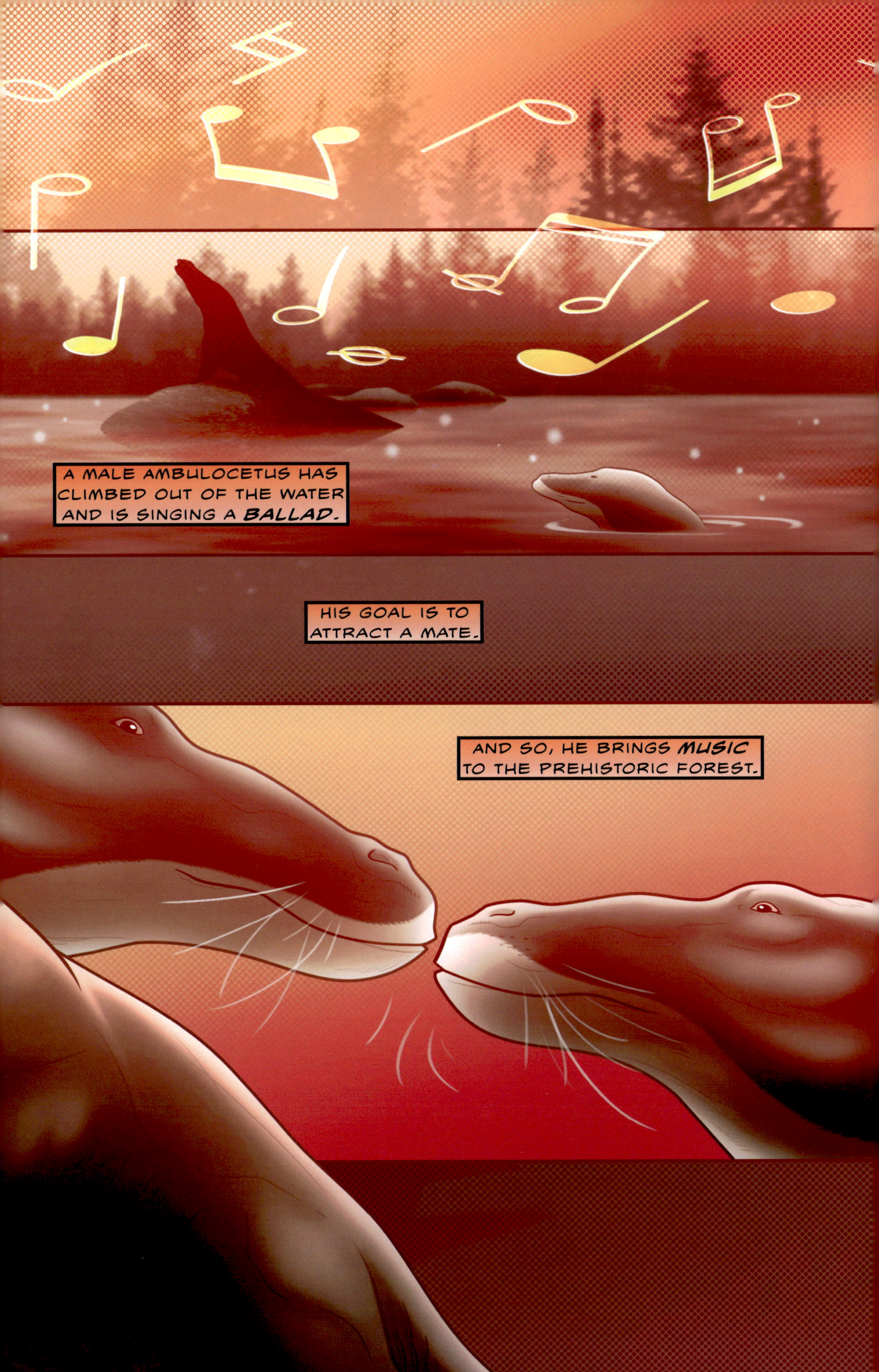

A MALE AMBULOCETUS HAS CLIMBED OUT OF THE WATER AND IS SINGING A *BALLAD*.

HIS GOAL IS TO ATTRACT A MATE.

AND SO, HE BRINGS *MUSIC* TO THE PREHISTORIC FOREST.

TODAY, WHALES BRING MUSIC TO THE SEAS.

THEIR HEART-STIRRING MELODIES ARE THE SOUNDTRACK TO THE DEEP.

BUT WITHOUT THEM —
THE SONG WOULD BE *SILENCED*.
THE DEEP WOULD GO QUIET.

THE MUSIC DOESN'T HAVE TO FADE TO BLACK.
THE SONG OF THE WHALE –
THE HOWL OF THE WOLF –
THE ROAR OF THE LION –
AND EVERY SQUEAK, CHIRP, AND CRY OF THE WILD –
IT'S UP TO ALL OF US.
PLEASE –
DON'T LET THE MUSIC BE TURNED OFF.

REXTOOTH
STUDIOS
REXTOOTH.COM

THE EARTH IS FOUR AND A HALF BILLION YEARS OLD.

COMPLEX LIFE DEVELOPED FIVE HUNDRED AND EIGHTY MILLION YEARS AGO.

IN THAT TIME OUR PLANET HAS BEEN HOME TO SOME TRULY AMAZING ANIMALS AND HAS BEEN THE STAGE FOR INCREDIBLE DRAMAS AND ADVENTURES.

REXTOOTH STUDIOS IS A PUBLISHER TELLING STORIES ABOUT THE AWESOME CREATURES THAT HAVE CALLED - AND STILL DO CALL - OUR PLANET HOME.

THE BOTTOM LINE IS REXTOOTH PRODUCES COOL STORIES WITH A FOCUS ON SCIENCE EDUCATION. THE MISSION STATEMENT IS AS SIMPLE AS THAT.